For my father. I'm thankful he bought a camp at Chesuncook Village and introduced me to the search for artifacts of the Abenaki. Years later, I wish I had paid closer attention.

Printed in the United States of America
First Printing, December 2020
ISBN 978-1-7339153-2-8
'Suncookers LLC, publisher

Suncookersworld.com

taussikerdesigns.com

The Nighthawk

Book two of the *'Suncookers* series

Author's Note

This is a story I have wanted to write for a long time, but *Tanglefoot* had to get out of the way first. The Abenaki stories are mostly true to form, but the talismans are my own creation.

I want to acknowledge Fanny Hardy Eckstrom's *The Penobscot Man.* Her retold story, "The Rescue," is the basis of Sam's Ride in Chapters 4-6.

Three fire rings did exist before the dams were built and were seen by Bruce Kenneson at the head of Chesuncook Lake at low water. A long time ago, a large village of Native Americans was the summer "Gathering Place." The village fulfills that same purpose centuries later.

"Plus ça change, plus c'est la même chose"
– Jean-Baptiste Alphonse Karr, 1849

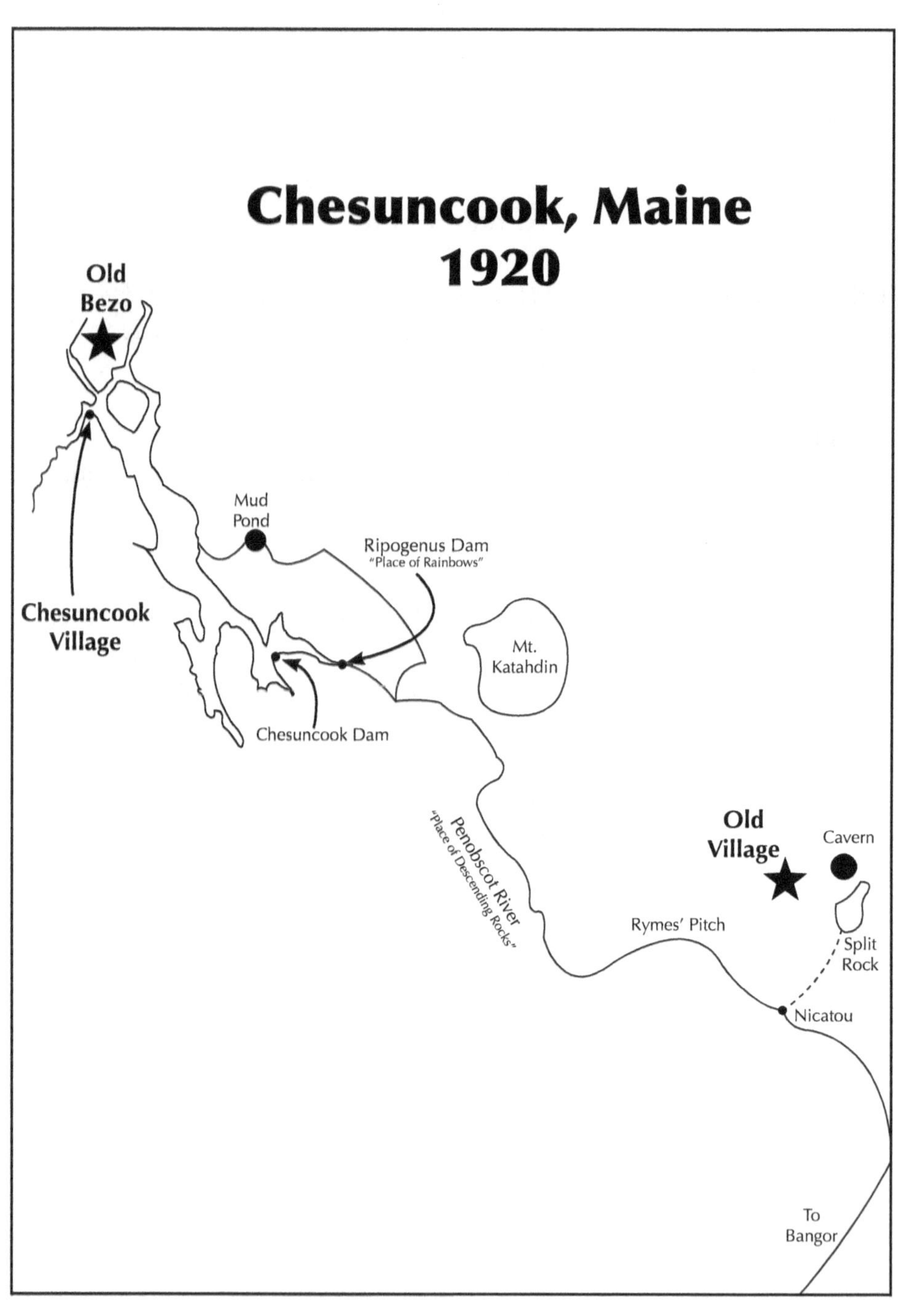

Chesuncook, Maine
1920
Old Bezo
Chesuncook Village
Mud Pond
Ripogenus Dam
"Place of Rainbows"
Mt. Katahdin
Chesuncook Dam
Penobscot River
"Place of Descending Rocks"
Old Village
Cavern
Rymes' Pitch
Split Rock
Nicatou
To Bangor

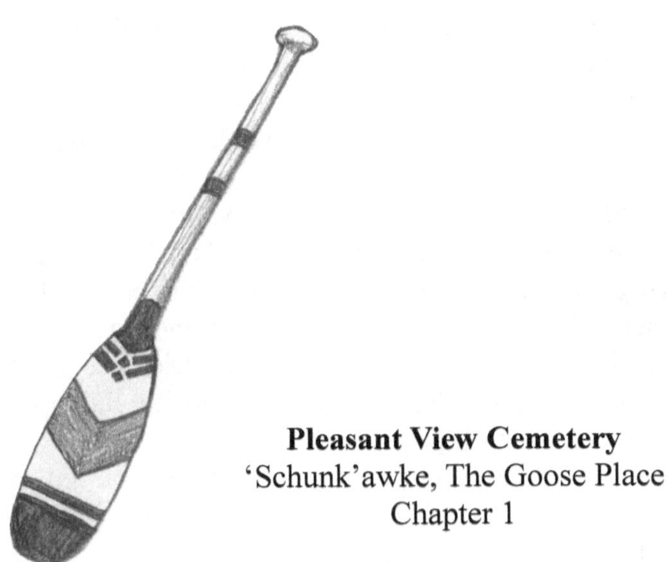

Pleasant View Cemetery
'Schunk'awke, The Goose Place
Chapter 1

Turning 50 last week was a milestone one doesn't usually seek, and it's over with pretty quick. Abby baked a birthday cake, and the kids made gave me useful presents they made themselves, a drying rack for mittens and gloves and an apple pie, my favorite. I was taking a moment to sit in the porch swing and gaze at Gero Island across the lake. The old farmhouses were all gone now, and just one large barn remained. The Indian reservation at the south end had been abandoned for years. I stared at the empty fields where hundreds of horses spent their summers. Time had not been kind to our small village. A few buildings had been victims of fire or rot, and most of the population of 'Suncookers, what the folks downriver called us residents of Chesuncook Village, had moved away since the Company was ending its logging operations using rivers and lakes. I began thinking about the day that everything changed when Abby and I, still teenagers, were doing some spring cleaning in the graveyard.

. . . .

"Charlie, help me with this headstone," came Abby's voice along the row of graves. I walked over, turned and paused at Mother's grave. 'Grace King,' the inscription that read, 'As you are now, so was I. As I am now, so you will be.' I had wanted her to have a pink granite heart that said simply, '*Mother*,' but Father wanted something more traditional. Instead of a pink heart, I was looking at a polished gray granite stone that looked much like the rest and not in any way signifying what she meant to me. You might remember hearing about the fire late last summer in the

Company's hotel our family managed. Our small village, in the middle of the Maine woods, catered to the logging business. We lost not only Mother in the fire but also my friend, Tommy. Coming to the Pleasant View cemetery to spruce things up wasn't a job I would have chosen for myself, but Abby insisted.

I was the only surviving son of the King family. My two brothers had been killed in the Great War, buried in some farmer's field in Verdun. My father, Caleb King, was a rum runner, and I was expected to help with the family business of making our signature moonshine, Tanglefoot. Abby and I had been friends for a while now, more than friends I should say. While he was working on a log drive in another state, her father had left her in care of his sister, the village school teacher.

"Charlie?" came a more urgent plea for my help. I buried my thoughts and again moved in her direction, but I wasn't moving fast enough for Abby. "Charlie!" Now she was shouting.

"Okay, I'm coming," I finally responded. Abby, the daughter of the famous river driver, Jim Ross, and I had been together since just before Mother died in the hotel fire. I miss Mother so much; Abby helped me through some dark days. She was trying to straighten an old and cracked slate headstone that Jack Frost had tumbled over last winter. The stone was a double one for the founders of the Gero family, both Taunt and Papa Gero. "Place the bar under here," I suggested. I pointed to the edge of the stone's cement base. "Now, press it down." While Abby pried by stepping on the bar, I pushed. The stone rose a little straighter each time we repeated the process, kicking bits of gravel under the raised edge when we pried it up.

It was the first day of May 1922, and I had just turned sixteen. The grass and weeds weren't growing this early in the season, but a winter's worth of fallen tree branches littered the cemetery's back fence. Cedar posts and a wire fence joined at a wrought iron gate. There were broken limbs draped over both.

I could see Mother's headstone the next row over. Being here wasn't easy for me. Some days, I couldn't bear the loss; the wound was still so raw. On those days, I'd get weepy just hearing her name.

"Making Pleasant View look nice just might help with the sadness I can see in your eyes at times," Abby said. I didn't know what to say to that. "Trust me, Charlie. Here, let's move this big branch." I came up beside her and helped drag off another large pine bough that had fallen during the winter. We tossed it over the fence out of sight.

I did trust her, and I loved her, too. Abby might be a little head strong at times, but that quality is what attracts me to her the most. I gathered up an armful of brush and came across a familiar headstone. "Margaret Ross," was chiseled in an arc across the rounded marble top. Below that was 'Beloved wife of Jim Ross.' According to the dates on the marble, she had died five years ago when I was ten and Abby was nine.

"Abby," I said. She stood up with an armful of sticks. I pointed at the gravestone. "That's the kind of stone I wanted for Mother." It was pink granite with a carved heart around her chiseled name and date.

She sighed, walked her armload of sticks a few steps to the back fence, and dumped them over. "It's a pretty stone, came all the way from Barre, Vermont. She died trying to have my brother," she said, walking back for another armful. "They're both there in the same coffin." Her dark brown eyes became watery.

"I remember the graveside service," I said. "Everyone in the village came. I'm really sorry you lost her." I looked in the direction of my mother's headstone, thinking about helping her in the kitchen. I'd give anything to have her nag me about not throwing my clothes everywhere.

"I really hate how time can pass so slowly," Abby said.

"What do you mean?" I asked.

"It seems like yesterday my mother was reading to me in the rocking chair by the parlor stove, my brother kicking inside her, the tree all decorated, stockings hung along the staircase and the smell of birthday cake baking in the oven. If I close my eyes, I can see us standing together lathering on the frosting and can almost taste the cake as if it had come out of the oven an hour before," she said wiping away a tear. "It's been years now, but it seems like minutes. Time seems to have stood still."

"It's not like it's time's fault," I said. "I don't think time slows down or speeds up unless we change how we look at all the things that happen to us. Mother's been gone over eight months now, but I don't want to think about it. I don't have any sense of time moving fast or slow."

"Know how you're really, really looking forward to something and then, when it happens, it seems it's over in an instant?" Abby asked. I did know. I remember looking forward to a birthday party so much, when it was over it felt like it flew by.

"Does seem like yesterday when my brothers came home from their special training," I said. "It was the last time I saw them."

"Do you remember the visit well?" Abby asked.

"I do," I said. "We had a lot of fun that last visit. They taught me some really great fighting moves. I wasn't big enough to bring them to the ground when we wrestled, but I did catch on with the staff when they taught me some of the special tricks they learned in their army survival school."

"Staff?" Abby asked.

"Just a straight stick about five feet long and as thick as my thumb. There were some tricky moves I did much better than they could because I was smaller, I think. Have you seen a bolo?" I asked. I didn't get an answer.

The wind rose, and the brown leaves of last fall blew up against the wire fence. When we heard a branch snap behind us, we turned to see a figure passing through the wrought iron gate. Hiram Francis was a Mic-Mac Indian from New Brunswick. He was a tribal shaman of sorts who lived with a flock of chickens at the southern end of the village. I watched his large frame loping across over fallen logs. His red plaid shirt and green wide brimmed felt hat made it easy to identify him at a distance.

"Mornin' Hi." Abby said. He walked closer to us, work gloves hanging from the back pocket of his coveralls, a shiny spade with a long handle over his shoulder.

"What brings you here? Got a job to do?" I asked. I really knew the answer. Hiram was the village grave digger, and his shovel gave away his errand.

"Sadly, I do," he replied. Mrs. Ames isn't doing so well, and her husband sent me up to get her resting spot ready. She isn't expected to last the night. With warm weather on the way, they won't be able to keep her in the camp for long." 'Suncookers could tell the weather by studying the sky, the wind and the clouds. Hot weather wasn't unusual this time of year, and after a long and brutally cold winter, we were looking forward to higher temps unless you wanted to keep a ripening corpse in your parlor for a few days of ceremony.

"Her family can't wait until her heart stops beating? Where are you going to put her?" Abby asked.

"They want her planted in their family lot along the back," pulling a small map from his back pocket, his handkerchief dragging along with it. Hiram blew his nose and stuffed the handkerchief back into his pocket. He unfolded the map. "Says lot number twenty, so that'd be over there between the Gero and Smart plots." Hiram pointed to a small area with no headstones sprouting from the greening sod. Hi walked over, re-checked his map, pacing off the distance from the stones on either side. He grabbed his shovel and began to peel the sod away from the black earth beneath but stopped after a few slices of the spade's sharp blade. Hiram stared at the stone across the row of graves.

"What are you staring at, Hi? I asked.

"See that headstone?" he asked, pointing to a tallish one a few feet away.

"I do," Abby said. "What's the figure carved into the top of the stone?" The stone wasn't new, but I hadn't paid any attention to it before. Now, I wish I hadn't examined it.

Hiram paused a moment. "That's the Nighthawk. He continued staring at the headstone.

"Ki'kwa'jenu?" Of all people, I should have known what it was. Ki'kwa'jenu was an evil spirit of Katahdin. I had been terrorized by its black wings and red eyes following me for some time in my dreams and in the dark as we found our way home from long trips to Bangor. It was there on the lakeshore after the boat explosion, waiting for me. It was as if I had something it wanted. I hadn't seen it for many months, and it had been absent from my dreams. Until now, was glad to have escaped its predatory presence.

"But why on that gravestone?" Abby asked. "Jim Whyte?" She referenced the name on the headstone. I stared at the carving, wondering why I hadn't noticed it before now.

"I thought I'd put those memories away," Hiram sighed. "And now they've returned. I have to ask why, but no one answers when I do."

"I think I remember him," I said. "Didn't he have a bit of a limp, large head and no neck?"

"That's Jim, alright," Hiram replied. "He had a cabin up Longley Stream once the new dam flooded everything out. An island at high water and a land bridge at low, the rock face where he built pointed into the prevailing winds enough to keep the flies at bay. Forested with tall pines, there was a carpet of blueberries happily turning sky blue over the brown bed of pine needles. Nestled in between grew winter mint, the teaberry plant of tiny red pumpkin shaped fruit hanging under the leaves if you cared to look.

"If anyone knew he was living on that little island, no one said. Squatting on Company property was discouraged. Jim was generous with his friends, and I think he knew someone in the main office he was able to pay off to keep his location a secret. No one really knew what he did for money, so there were lots of rumors. Some thought he smuggled opium using the train along the gorge just up north. He made trips to the village every couple of weeks, and sometimes your father would bring him down the lake. Jim would go down river to Bangor and not return for a month. When he did re-appear at the Dam for a boat ride back up the lake, he was driving a brand-new Marmon model 34 with a V8.”

"Isn't that the car kept in the barn beside the storage building for our Tanglefoot?” I asked. "I remember peeking in the knotholes to see it when I was a kid.”

"That's the one,” Hiram said. "And it's still there, too.”

"Didn't he have any family?” Abby asked.

"Not that anyone knew about,” Hiram explained. "He owned a small lumber mill in Miller's Falls, but then there was a tragic accident.”

"What happened?” Abby asked.

"Jim disappeared one morning while he was at his saw mill. He was checking the shredder they used to mince up the slab wood from the sawing. The Company bought the ground pulp for paper. Most folks thought he slipped and fell in. The grinders must have pulled him apart.” Hiram paused to let the image sink in. "The mill kept running that morning. There wasn't anything to clean up. He was pretty well mixed in with the morning's ground wood. Folks wondered about the paper made from that ground wood pulp that was seasoned with Jim. Did the paper make its way for a legal contract, or had it become the obituary notices in the Bangor Currier?”

"But no one saw it happen? Abby asked.

"No, there were no witnesses, just one of his fancy shoes left on the grate at the top of the shredder.”

"I don't get why the Nighthawk is on his stone. There's no body buried underneath, right?” I asked.

"No body, just a memorial stone. Jim made a deal with the devil,” Hiram said. "The woman who came back with him from one trip told me about it. She said he was plagued by the Nighthawk following him everywhere, in his dreams every night. She said Jim felt the beast wanted something from him, but he didn't know what. Jim had every success, stepping on a few toes on the way, but one morning Old Scratch came to collect.”

"How'd he get the money to buy the Marmon?” I asked. "It must have cost over five thousand dollars!” Father had some magazines and I would pour over the ads for the latest car. The Marmon was the most expensive one I read about.

"That's about right. The rumor was that he was making drug deals in New Jersey. The train would pass over the Chamberlain Gap on its way from Quebec. Jim would signal from an overlook, and a package would be tossed out at a certain spot. Jim would hike down to retrieve it, then get it south to turn it into cash. He always had a lot of cash as I recall." Hiram stood up. He seemed to be done with reminiscing for now. "Some say he buried gold and jewels where he was squatting at Longley in one of the caves there but no one has ever found anything."

"Maybe we should go look for it," Abby said. "What cave?"

"There's a cave near the top of Caucmagomic Mountain. You know where the eagles have their nest?" Hiram said.

"I've never been there." That was one place I had never explored.

"We should go sometime," Abby said. Hiram pulled out his handkerchief and wiped his brow. It was already getting warm as the sun streamed into the cemetery's clearing.

"Fiddleheads are ready. Going picking tomorrow." He began to remove the sod on Mrs. Ames' final resting place, stacking it neatly along the short end of the grave. "Weather coming off warm next few days, so tomorrow will be the last chance. See you there?"

"We'll be there," Abby said. And we turned and began the short walk back to the village along out the little rutted path to the main road, another wagon path but a bit wider.

Our small logging village has a one-lane gravel road. The road isn't long and doesn't go anywhere, just meandering from house to house along three miles of homes, camps and shanties. We could see Gero Island, barely a mile across the lake. Gero wasn't an island before Rip Dam was built a few years ago, flooding out some of the village. Four farms with vast fields surrounding each.

"Look, Charlie," Abby said, jerking me out of my reverie. "The kids have a maypole." Abby pointed down the lane leading past the schoolhouse where school children were dancing around a decorated pole, blue and yellow crepe paper winding around it.

"Remember when we used to do that?" I asked.

"I used to tease you a lot," Abby reminded me. "You know it's because I liked you, right?" She smiled.

"I thought you did then, but that was in the third grade," I replied. I don't remember much about those early school days. Her dad was away directing some log driving out West. Meanwhile, Abby's aunt, the village schoolteacher boarded with us at the Katahdin View and looked after her. Abby wasn't in my class for more than a couple of months at a time before her father pulled her out because of where he was working. Until the winter of '20, I hadn't seen her for nearly six years. When we did run into each other again, it was late one night two winters ago when Tommy and I were icing the tote roads with the sprinkler.

Men and horses moved big pine logs from the woods on iced-over tote roads to the shores of rivers and lakes in the winter. In the spring they'd be flushed down the waterways to the mills. Tommy and I would drive the sprinkler at night, a giant barrel on a sled, dribbling water on those trails, making it easier to slide heavy loads to their destination. The tote-roads were mostly unusable when the snow and ice was gone. Abby was going the wrong way on a one-way tote road. To keep horses and men safe, all the tote roads were one-way, and there were "haul-back" roads for the empty return trip. A team of horses pulling a load of logs down icy hills wouldn't do well meeting something coming at them. When Abby flew by us that night, nearly crashing into us, I had no idea who she was. After her mother died, Abby and her father went out west. Her father was still there, showing Oregon how wood was run down the rivers. Then, not able to keep her safe from the leers of some of the men, he sent her back to Chesuncook where his sister looked after her.

"They look like they're having fun," she said. Children were dancing and giggling around the Maypole. It was too early for flowers way up here in the land of ice and snow , but paper daisies encircled a young girl's head here and there. From a distance, Miss Ross kept an eye on the celebration, the brass recess bell in her hand.

"I remember Miss Ross telling us how old the maypole dance was," I said.

"I think it's mostly about making braids as the dancers weave their ribbons around the pole," Abby pointed out.

"I thought it was more about how time ties our lives together," I said.

"What does a maypole have to do with time?" Abby asked.

"Time is interwoven with everything we do. It isn't a separate thing," I explained. "The ribbons are the many timelines that we create when we make even the simplest decisions."

"You think too much! You know that, right?" Abby teased. I just nodded my head. Timelines and all those "what-if's" really confused me, and I needed to change the conversation.

"Yeah, I guess I do. I remember seeing oxen dragging the schoolhouse up here from Graveyard Point." I said.

Years ago, the combined one-room schoolhouse, town hall and church had been dragged up from the lakeshore by teams of oxen. It had been built on Company land, but the Company wanted the graves moved so they could build a logging depot with bunk houses and a storehouse. So everyone was dug up and replanted at the new Pleasant Hill cemetery. The schoolhouse/townhall's final resting place, set beside the path to the village cemetery, was on a little rise across a grassy driveway we were now walking down. Its square tower with cupola faced the lake. The diamond shaped windows on either side, positioned half-way to the top, were really square ones turned on their points, an architectural feature found mostly in New England.

"I was out west with my father then. Last time I was in the building was when it was next door to the Inn. Let's look inside," Abby said.

"Not long," I cautioned. "Remember we promised Olive we'd be there to help by nine." The drive had started, and a few men had already checked in. This morning they were rolling logs into the river just below Pine Stream Falls. Olive was expecting us to help with making and serving meals farm table style, to eight or nine starving men.

While the students were dancing around the maypole, Abby and I went inside. Abby's Aunt was watching the kids outside, and she waved to us as we went up the steps. The building was empty. Morning light streamed through the old wavy panes of glass down to the entryway, in front of heavy double wooden doors that were swung wide open into the hall. Dust motes were floating in the sun's rays. Beyond the doors we saw rows of chairs and desks lined up at the sides, leaving a center aisle that ended at a slightly raised dais on which stood a lectern. A well-worn bible rested there, opened to the closing verses of last Sunday's service. A foot-pumped organ sat off to the right, facing the congregation.

"I heard a story about Danny Gero dunking Rose's pigtail," Abby giggled.

"How could I forget that scene?" I said. Abby was out west with her father then. We stood looking at the inkwell and pen tray along the flat part of the wooden chair-desk. The ink well would hold a small glass jar of black ink to use with the steel nib pens that were kept in the trays when students were practicing their penmanship. Rose Gero, Danny's cousin, had the prettiest light blond hair in two long pigtails down her back. Danny lifted one of her pigtails and dipped it into the ink well, the mouth of which was just wide enough for a good dunking. When Rose felt a little tug, she jumped up. Seeing what Danny had done, Rose swatted him with it, black ink spraying everywhere. It was quite a mess. Danny and Rose became good friends later on, though.

"Looks like another crew heading up the river," Abby pointed out. Looking northwest, we could see boats navigating the channel between two piers that framed the mouth of the Upper West Branch where it entered Chesuncook Lake. These piers sat on each side of the steep banks of the riverbed. The bottom logs of each pier were now exposed since the water level was so low. Sluice gates at Rip had been opened to flush the wood down river most of the summer and fall before. These gates closed when the last of the wood was flushed down river. Around ice-out at the end of April, the water level would rise again, putting the tops of most piers even with the high water. Neither melting snow nor spring rains had refilled the lake this April. My Uncle Amos said this might become a drought year. Flushing pulpwood down the rivers would be a challenge until the rains came.

Goosegrass Flats, a low, muddy shelf where geese often congregated, was just to the west of the river's small delta. Remains of several foundations poked up through the mud. You could see broken glass, rusty parts of wood stoves, and the remains of rock walled wells when the water was this low. Several houses had been dragged away by teams of horses and oxen. One home floated between the village cove and Gero Island and back again several times until my Uncle Amos tied it up to a tree in front of the little store he ran. When the owners of the now submerged lot didn't return to claim the house, residents of Gero Island towed it across the lake and hauled it up to the field's edge for their schoolhouse. A few years later, it got dragged back. Very little was thrown out in this remote settlement.

We walked back to the "new" King residence, the last house on the way to Graveyard Point. Our place was an Acadian style house with three large peaks on the sides and two along the front. There were a dozen bedrooms, two parlors, a huge kitchen and a dining hall. There was a wrap-around porch, supports painted in three colors with wide railings. Built to house logging crews, it gave the Company's hotel a little competition until the fire. We could get to the barn through a long, connecting shed where the summer kitchen was set up and firewood was stacked. The shed also housed a chopping block for kindling and chickens, the privy, and at the very end, the tackle shop for the horses and oxen we used in the woods and fields. The house pointed directly at Mt. Katahdin, Maine's highest peak. It seemed right to name it the Katahdin View Inn.

My stepmother, Olive, met us at the door.

"Leave those boots outside!" she yelled, seeing us climb up the porch steps. "I've mopped this floor for the third time today, and it's only nine o'clock!"

"Okay," I yelled back, and Abby and I sat on the deacon's bench just outside the entry way and shucked off our boots. "You'd think she'd get used to dirt getting tracked in," I said.

"Come on, Charlie, we have to do our part to help keep the Inn clean. It's not much to ask, is it?" Abby stowed her boots under the bench beside mine.

"You two are just in time to knead the bread and bring in more firewood. Got a lot of baking to do today," Olive said. "I've got to get these beans soaking so they'll be ready for tomorrow night's supper." We had beans every Saturday night. Never failed. Olive used the smaller pea sized beans and an old bean pot Hiram had found in the hotel's ashes. The beans were always good, but a ham or a chicken would have been a welcome change from her menu's routine.

Olive was teaching us the old language. She would be sure we could say the words with the right tone. She would often quiz us while we were washing dishes as she sat down for probably the first time of the day, nursing a cup of coffee.

"Beaver," she'd say.

"Tomakwa," we'd reply in unison, competing to see who could say it first.

"M'teoulin," Olive shouted out,

"Magic," Abby replied.

"Goose Place," she'd say.

"Gesoncook," we'd reply. 'Gesoncook' is one of the old names of our lake and village, Chesuncook. Sometimes she would call it 'Schunk'awke,' as if she were honking like a goose. The sound was more important than the spelling, we learned. The language was hard to put on paper. There could be several spellings of the same word. The good thing about all our lessons of Abenaki language was that both of us had a good ear and remembered the pronunciations.

"You're both speaking the old language well," she said from her chair at the little kitchen table, her black eyes twinkling. Olive's round face and high cheekbones, her dark hair and eyes, and her brown skin were all screaming "Wabanaki," or "People of the Dawnland." Her ancestors had lived on this land for thousands of years. She stood and smoothed her apron. "We have to get the bread going. Here's the dough."

Olive took a large yellow bowl from the warming oven and dumped the dough on a well-floured cutting board. Abby started kneading, and I went out to get more stove wood. After I filled the wood box and Abby had the buttered loaves in the oven, we sat down with Olive at the kitchen table.

"Any woodsmen coming in this week?" I asked. Father would bring them up the lake from the Dam in his 'new' boat, *Twilight*. His beloved *Tethys* had been destroyed in an explosion, killing seventeen woodsmen the year before.

"Your father did say he was bringing some people up, but they're not all woodsmen," Olive said, her brow furrowed with disapproval.

"Who do you think they are?" Abby asked.

"What I think about his business doesn't matter." Olive usually had an opinion, but not this time.

"When we were in the cemetery this morning, Hiram told us a story of Jim Whyte. Did you ever meet him?" I asked.

"I surely did," Olive replied, a smile on her face replacing her furrowed brow of disapproval. "He was a good looker, Jim was. And kind and generous, too, for a white man. I was really sweet on him, at least until I met your father. Too bad about what happened. He didn't deserve to go that way."

Those few words told me a lot. Olive clearly saw herself as Native American. She defined white men as being neither generous nor kind. It made me wonder what she saw in Father.

"Do you think his camp at Longley is still standing?" I asked.

"I've never seen it."

"Some may still be left, but it was a temporary place at best. Maybe you could find the treasure." Olive stirred another lump of sugar into her coffee.

"Treasure?" I asked. "What's that about?"

"I heard that from a good friend who used to go over to 'visit' with him, if you know what I mean. She said that Jim didn't trust banks and hid his money. There was one place, he told me, where no one would ever look."

"Where?" I asked.

"High on a cliff where there was an eagle's nest in the mouth of a cave."

"Now the snow's gone," Abby said, "we could look for it."

"Better busy yourselves with readying the rooms upstairs first," Olive said. "Guests will be here this afternoon, and there's the bread, too." She got up and put her cup in the sink. "I'm going out to dig in the garden. The dough should be kneaded again." Shedding her plaid gingham apron, she grabbed a pair of gloves, and as she went out the back door she said, "Come out to help after you've finished. Those weeds are growing faster than I can pull them up." After checking on the bread rising on the counter, Abby and I went to work making up the rooms.

I was pretty tired when I went to bed that night and fell asleep the second my head hit the pillow. Visions of weeds and pea sprouts danced about. The only dream I remember was about a cave, a fire and a bear. I was being chased. The bear nearly caught up to me as I ran through orange flames. Each time the bear got closer. Sometimes I had dreams of Ki'kwa'jenu's black wings carrying me away. The Nighthawk was always present, just out of sight in the shadows. Abby made me promise that I'd tell her whenever I dreamed of him again. But I didn't always remember. Bad things always happened when I forgot.

Fiddleheadin'
Chapter 2

The next day, Abby and I were out looking for fiddleheads. These ferns sprout in May and grow to two or three inches high. They're delicious with a nice nutty flavor. First you have to remove the little paper sheath, and then you steam them. Serve them with a juicy steak, and oh, my! Or other foraging option this time of year was dandelion greens, and neither of us liked the greens. We found a patch of fiddleheads and began picking. Soon we had one of our pack baskets half full. When I stood up to stretch, I spied Hiram walking along the side of the old stream cut where we were foraging.

"Good fiddleheadin' up here," Hi announced, asserting his knowledge of all things fern-like.

"I know," I said back.

"We've one basket half full," said Abby looking down into the basket. "I think that's enough. We still have to clean all these."

Hiram stood and stared at us. He seemed to be studying our faces. "Your grandmothers are Beothuk Indians. Not just you, Charlie, but you, too." He pointed at Abby.

"That's right," she said. "Grandmother Molly is a member of the Neptune family, I think the Otter Clan."

I stared at her. "Why didn't you tell me before?" She just smiled at me. I could never argue with one of Abby's smiles. I wondered what other secrets Abby held close.

"She isn't just in the Neptune family," Hiram offered. "Awasosqua is a powerful chief of her people. I know some about the Beothuks and

21

Norembegas, mostly gone from this earth."

"Awasosqua? That's 'mother bear.' What can you tell me about my Grandmother Molly? I met her only a few times, and that was a long time ago."

Hiram looked at her. "I know her pretty well. She and I have spent a lot of time together over the years, and…"

"You're together?" Abby interrupted. Now, this was real news to me, too.

"You could say that, when she isn't in one of her obstinate, mule-headed moods."

"I had no idea," she said. The surprise on her face had turned into an approving smile. Hiram was an important part of my life, and I could tell that Abby had the same respect for him that I had. He was like a grandfather to me, and now he's practically a real grandfather to Abby.

"Awasosqua has a certain power. She uses it from time to time to bring the deer or summon the fish when times are hard. She wore the amulet of the spirit of Katahdin." I sensed that Hiram knew a lot more about Grandmother Molly. His voice softened when he said her name, and I could tell that he cared about her.

"Amulet?" Abby asked. Hiram thought for a moment.

"There's a story of the mountain spirit and his new bride," Hi said. He put his pack basket on a nearby log and sat down. "Katahdin gave her a golden amulet One day, the new bride wanted to surprise her husband with a meal of fern sprouts, like these fiddleheads." Hiram pointed to his pack basket on the log beside him.

"She found lots, but they were all the wrong kind. She got too close to a cliff and slipped off, falling to her death on the rocks below. The only thing the mountain spirit found where she had fallen was that amulet. If you held it up to the sun or in front of a potlatch fire like we used to have here every year, it would light up. Katahdin's new bride disappeared into the spirit realm, and her earthly form followed. The amulet was a way to summon powers of Katahdin. All the tribes know that story. That amulet was a gift to your people from the great spirit."

"Is that the same one I remember Grandmother Molly wearing?" Abby asked.

"Look for some pictures of her when she was young. I'm certain that you'll see her wearing it," Hi said. "She had M'teoulin".

"You mean 'magic'?" Abby said. I nodded my head in agreement.

"How do you know the word?" Hiram asked. "Very few know what it means."

"Olive has been teaching us the old language," Abby explained.

Hiram nodded. "It's important to pass that on, or the old language will be only on our maps as names of lakes and rivers," Hiram replied.

"There's more to it than just words. If you ever see the cave beyond Split Rock, you'll find figures carved in the walls, petroglyphs, the archaeologists call them, mostly of deer, moose and bear. I remember seeing a woolly mammoth carved into the floor when I was there last."

"Abby's grandmother is a shaman?" I asked.

"Many come to her for her ability to cure the sick. She was the tribal doctor and was good at it. Once you meet her, you'll never forget her." Hiram hefted his basket over his shoulders, fiddleheads inside.

"It's time to get these cooking," Hiram announced, and he began walking home. His green felt hat slowly blended in with the fir and spruce as he disappeared into the woods.

Abby looked at me. "I think we should look for a photo. There might be one in the safe in the clerk's office. Dad keeps some family papers there. Let's head back by the Boom House and I can check."

I followed her long stride on the path. Even though Abby was a few inches shorter, her strong legs could cover a lot of ground fast, her flaming red hair bouncing behind her. It wasn't long before we came to the trail, wide enough for a Model A, that led to the upper Boom House. In several spots, blueberry bushes were beginning to bud. It could be a great berry year if we got some rain soon. We turned into the grassy yard where the clerk's office sat not far from the West Branch. No one mowed the lawn. Instead, the cook moved the goat tie-out to a different spot each morning.

I sat on the little porch while Abby went inside. She told the clerk what she needed. Soon, she came outside with a large manila envelope. The clerk was at the window watching us, his beady eyes darting here and there.

"Did you get them?" I asked.

"Think I have them all. Let's go, I don't like being here the way that clerk looks at me." I helped her with the pack, stained a dark brown with porcupine quills woven in a diamond shaped designs for decoration. When we started along the path in the woods, I saw the clerk turn away from the window.

"Where'd you get that basket?" I asked after her. "I've seen a lot of pack baskets, but I haven't seen one as nice. It looks like an old design. It looks a little like Hiram's."

"My dad gave it to me," answered Abby. "He did say that it was based on an old design. He got it from Hiram, I think. Something about 'being in the family,' but I never understood what that meant until now. Besides, Dad isn't around much these days so I can ask him."

"That's hard for you, isn't it?" I asked her. "I know you really miss him."

"Yeah, but time passes, doesn't it? Whether you want it to or not. I've gotten used to not seeing him much. He does write once in a while. I just hope he's okay," Abby said. Her father had left Abby under his sister's care. Miss Ross had moved out of Bill's Boarding House when Pete shot Bill's chicken killing dog in Bill's front yard. Seems the dog found his way under Pete's chicken fencing. All that was left of the flock was one frightened rooster and a yard full of feathers. When Pete fired his muzzle loader, the bullet screamed into the closet where Abby's aunt was hiding, splintering the wood right behind Miss Ross's ear.

We didn't have time to look at the pictures when we got back. The fiddleheads had to be cleaned or they would spoil. Dinner had to be made. There were guests to look after, and Olive was giving us another lesson in speaking the old Wabenaki language while we were working in the kitchen. It seemed Olive's mission in life to preserve her language by teaching it to two captive students. We were getting pretty good at speaking it.

After Olive left the kitchen to check in some late arriving guests, Abby and I stood side by side in front of the double Monson slate sink, slate drain boards on each side, working on a pile of dishes. I could tell that something was bothering her.

"You seem lost in your thoughts," I said, as I finished scrubbing a large platter.

"It's just a dream I've been having. It bothers me mostly because it doesn't seem to be related to anything," Abby said. "Here, let me take that." Abby reached for the platter in my hand, giving it a quick rinse and placing it on the shelf above.

"Dreams usually tell us something," I cautioned as she stared out the little window above the sink that faced the huge pine tree on the point.

"It's about a bear," Abby said. "It's chasing after me and it's gaining ground."

I remembered my bear dream. Now Abby had one? "What happens?"

"I always wake up just before it gets me." She looked at me as if I had the answer to the dream's origin.

I nodded my head. "I've had a dream something like that. I wake up at the very moment his claws grab me." I handed Abby a serving plate to put away. "What are the chances we both have dreams of bears? Why not moose?"

"Maybe it's because we were both talking about bears that evening? I don't know. Dreams are strange," she said. "Sometimes I have the same one again and again. My father told me it's because there's a big change happening in my life. I could never figure out what the change was, though. Maybe it's you?" She looked up at me and smiled. I smiled back

"Nice to think so," I said. "Sometimes I have the same dreams over and over, too. If it's not about a bear grabbing me, then I'm falling out of the canoe and nearly drowning in the whitewater," I offered. I handed her another plate. I was quiet for a moment, letting the last two days events drift through my mind. Abby was just as quiet, and I think she was doing the same.

"Now you're the one lost in thought," Abby said as she put her hand on my shoulder.

"Just thinking about the last two days, the cemetery, my mother, the stories Hiram told us, M'teoulin." Then I thought of Abby's Grandmother. "Do you remember anything about your grandmother's amulet?" I asked.

Abby sighed. "Not very much. It was nearly transparent with a light-yellow tint. When you held it up to the sun, it just glowed it was so pretty. She never said anything about it, but she always wore it around her neck."

We finished cleaning the ferns. It wasn't until after dinner dishes had been washed and put away that we could sit down to look at the contents of the large brown envelope she had taken from the Company's safe. Inside were a dozen or so very old photos. There was a name on the back of each one.

Abby handed me a photo. "This is Grandmother Molly when she was much younger." When I looked at the photo, I thought I was looking at Abby. Her grandmother's face had the same oval shape, the same high cheekbones, the same almond shaped eyes and thick eyebrows nearly meeting in the middle. She wore a tall, silk hat with a brim, widest over her ears, and with a decorative band that squeezed the top of the hat into a plume. Around her neck was a black necklace embedded with porcupine quills in diamond designs. Below that, a round amulet hung right above a cross. Her black, wavy hair went down her shoulders to her elbows. Her cape was embroidered with beads and ribbons.

Abby shuffled through some other photos, turning over one to see the name. "This is one of my uncles, John Merry." She handed it to me as I returned the picture of her grandmother.

"He was the governor of the tribe," Abby told me. Dressed conservatively like most men, his long hair, high cheekbones and the same almond eyes of Abby's all gave away his ancestry.

"We should go see her," Abby said. "It's been too long since my last visit. You know, lately I've had the feeling that she's calling to me, but I don't know why. It's really odd."

"Where does she live?"

"Her ndakina is Nicatou Island. My father took me there a couple of times."

"Her what?" I asked.

"Ndakina," Abby repeated. "Remember? It means 'homeland.'"

"Do you think you could find her place again?" I asked.

"I remember where it was on the island. She lived in a log cabin. I'd remember it if I saw it again."

"If we go, we'll have to make plans for someone to help Olive run the Inn," I suggested. I didn't think Abby should go alone. It was a long trip down river. She'd need another paddler for the whitewater and to help with carrying the canoe and gear around the rougher rapids and falls.

"Okay," she said. "Let's ask someone. I have to ask my aunt, but I know she'll say it's okay to go. Maybe your father would haul us down the lake on his way to pick up more river drivers. Do you think he'll be alright without you at the still?"

"I'll ask him when he gets home," I said. "He had a lot of cargo to ferry to the Depot; he'll be back after dark with Louis to unload our supplies." Louis Maki had been helping us with the 'shine business since last summer. Now that Tommy was in Pleasant Hill beside his brother, Father needed another pair of hands with making and transporting cases of Tanglefoot, the King family signature moonshine. Customers said it was the best in New England.

We cleaned up for the evening. Father came in, drank the neck and shoulders off a bottle of Tanglefoot, and went upstairs before I had a chance to ask about a ride. There were days that he didn't say much to me. He must have his own demons to wrestle, I thought. Rum running was picking up again, and I could just see him debating the risks, doing everything he could to prevent another deadly attack on his family.

Since Mother had died in the hotel fire the year before, all of us were watching out for the Boston gang in case they decided to make another visit. Father, Uncle Amos and Louis wore sidearms now, telling anyone who asked that the firearm was only to discourage bears. Just last month I overheard a discussion between Uncle Amos and Father about guns and smuggling people. It looked like they had given up the idea of a potato farm in Aroostook County.

Abby was on the phone looking for someone to help Olive while we were away, and I would have to be up early to ask Father in the morning. I went to my room and fell asleep to the cries of loons fishing along the lakeshore. Visions of golden amulets haunted my dreams that night.

Whitewater
Chapter 3

Abby arranged for some help at the Inn while we were gone. Louis Maki was going to put in some extra time working with Uncle Amos in the barn, and Louis' wife, Anna, would help Olive in the kitchen. Her baby boy was a few months old, and Olive was looking forward to the visit. Father brought us down the lake. He was expecting to return with a crew of Bangor Tigers, a rough bunch of seasoned rivermen who would do almost anything for a dollar. We had our gear and food packed for a week of travel, two extra paddles and two long poles. The 18-foot canoe, made on the Templeton mold, slid behind us on a taut bowline behind the *Twilight*. That mold, a wooden frame around which the cedar strips were bent and tacked together, produced a canoe that was lightweight, strong and suitable for both flat and whitewater.

The Katahdin Range seemed to grow much larger as we approached Weymouth Point. OJI, Double Top and Sourbungee were all in the clear, but thick, black clouds wrapped around Pomola and Wichowen, opposite peaks and opposing spirits of Katahdin. The weather was about to change, and not for the better.

Soon, we could hear rolls of thunder above the noise of the engine. We could see lightning forking over Firecracker Alley, a section between the river and the foothills of Katahdin on the Abol side where so many fires had been caused by lightning strikes. Our canoe trip would take us right beside the old burn.

Now, the lake turned to a darker shade of slate, the rising wind whipping up white caps that were looked pretty pointed. It wouldn't be long before the white curtain of rain we could see in the distance passed

29

over us. We put on our rain gear and rubber boots. The thunderheads were turning and even darker gray.

Father pointed the *Twilight* between two islands, careful to stay in the middle of the channel. I could have hit either island with a rock if I wanted, they were so close. Then, a single bolt of lightning struck just off the bow, the bolt splitting in two just above us, each fork hitting the islands on each side of us. Rocks and sticks came hurtling through the alders and brush at the river's edge, the water pockmarked with the debris, a few chunks of loosened earth crashing against the side of the boat. Fish jumped all around. The bolt splitting in two, the crash of thunder, the rocks shredding the brush, and all the fish jumping out of the water....all happened in the same two seconds. The smell of the lightning hung in the air.

"Jesus Christ on a bicycle!" Father shouted, his knuckles white on the steering wheel. "Damn near pissed my pants!"

I could see Abby turn away to hide her laughter.

After Father left us at Rip Dam, Abby and I loaded the canoe into the back of a wagon Father had arranged for us to use. We waited on the Boom House porch for the rain to let up. After the storm, we drove two Belgian horses around Ripogenus Rapids, past the gorge and Cribworks. We left the horses and wagon with the camp clerk there. The Belgians would be boarded until we returned. After unloading our gear at the water's edge, we slid the canoe partly in the water and began to load it. The wind had dropped off, and a soft mist hung in the air.

Satisfied that we had a balanced load, we pushed off the river's edge into the eddy current. The canoe slid easily over the slime covered rocks. The air smelled fresh after the storm passed. I took the bow and Abby sat in the stern. She knew how to steer a canoe through whitewater, and she was a really good paddler. I knew how to read the water ahead and call out which direction we should be steering. The water was faster after the recent rain in spite of a mild drought that began the month with little snow melt from an open winter. There would be more rocks than water, was my guess, but I was wrong. I didn't have much time to decide which way we were going to paddle. The river had started to rise, not a lot, but enough to quicken the pace of our trip. Some alders along the river's edge had their feet in the water. I had to keep out a sharp eye for the V's and the pour-overs, the sounds of rushing water getting louder as we approached. Once or twice, we had to eddy out behind a large rock just to rest. A sharp focus was essential.

There's an old river driver's saying: "Go to the left of the rock, to the right of the rock, and if you delay or don't decide, you'll be sitting on top of the rock." There were a lot of rocks ahead. I didn't have a chance to relax and enjoy the trip. "Left," I shouted, or "Right." Sometimes we had to ferry backward, sliding the canoe over to one side of the river or to the other. We did this by paddling backwards while "drawing" or pulling water to the side. It was a lot of work.

We paddled hard, riding over the three clear tongues of water at Amberjackamockamus. We coasted through the horseraces below, dodging the exposed rocks there. I could see an eagle's nest high in the pines above Nesourdnahunk while we paddled the deadwater. Soon, we arrived at the mouth of Salmon Stream where we had our lunch. When we continued on our way, I could see Katahdin poking its head out of the clouds.

The river began to narrow, and the current seemed much stronger. The smoke was much heavier now, and I could barely see the little takeout beach above the falls. Where the river began to narrow, we heard the roar of the river cascading over a sharp ledge. Just ahead, I could see water spitting up into the air, smooth waves turning into whitecaps, but because of the smoke, I could see nothing beyond it. We were getting too close to the falls

"We've got to ferry to the left side. Now!" I shouted, drawing my paddle to the left, while Abby drew to the opposite side, getting the canoe in an angle to the current while keeping it stable. We spun the canoe around, so it was pointed up stream. I reached out with my paddle and grabbed some still eddy current next to the shore, drawing us in behind a rock jutting out just above the low ledge beside us. It was a good thing we could take the canoe out here.

"That was close," I shouted over the roar of the falls just ahead.

"Keep a good grip on that ledge!" Abby nodded her head. Her mouth was moving, but I couldn't hear her.

"What?" I yelled at her.

"Hurry up! I can't hold on much longer," she shouted back. "I don't want to swim these falls!" I stepped out of the canoe, turned and grabbed the side. Then Abby stepped out onto the wet ledge and tied the bow of the canoe to a nearby alder bush that grew in a crevasse of otherwise solid rock.

The roar of the falls was deafening. In a few minutes, we emptied the canoe and hauled it out of the water, lifting it over our heads and began the carry over big gray rocks.

"Hold it," Abby yelled from under the bow. The canoe was

resting on our shoulders, our heads inside. It took a while, but soon the canoe was safely resting on a sandy beach at an eddy below the falls. We had to make three more trips for the rest of the gear.

....

Nesoudnahunk Falls, a twelve-foot drop, was right around the corner where we couldn't see, but we could surely hear. The only boatmen to have paddled the falls successfully were Big Sabattus Mitchell and his crew of Mic-Macs seventy-five years ago. According to the tale, it was a close call. Indians would be together in one bateau, white men in the rest. Some had already started the carry around the falls, heavy bateaux cutting into their shoulders while they barked their shins on the 'big grays,' giant granite boulders that made up the path. Sabat's crew was the last to pull out of the river, but his men stopped just at the edge of the bank when they heard him say, "Let's run this, boys." They looked ahead where the other crews were just out of sight down the carry path. Then they looked back at Sabat and all nodded their heads. Polling their bateaux back into the current, they paddled the smooth tongue of the falls and disappeared over the edge.

"Look at that!" They would not have heard the others cry out from shore. The noise of the rapids was so loud. When they pulled into an eddy out of sight just below the rest of the men, Sabat's brave crew had time to splash the water out of the boat with their paddles unobserved. When the other crews ran down to see the condition of the boat, it appeared that Sabat's men had had an easy time of it. There was little water in the boat. When they turned over the boat to examine the bottom, there wasn't a mark.

The other crews had just finished carrying their heavy bateaux around the falls. They felt challenged by the success of Sabat's run. In an effort to prove they could run the falls even better than Sabat, the men carried their boats back up the trail to the upper eddy above the rapids. One died in their attempt to navigate the whitewater. All the boats were smashed to pieces.

....

When we got to the little beach below the falls, I realized this must be the same eddy where Sabat's crew found safety. I thought about the men who died there, and for what, I wondered. Pride had killed more than one river driver over the years, but the greatest danger was a little slip of the foot when running across logs bobbing in the current.

The wind shifted, then calmed. Now, it was coming from

behind us. We paddled on past Little Nesourdnahunk Stream and into Abol Deadwater. There was some current here, but not a lot. Several moose were grazing on water lilies, and loons fished on one side while a family of mergansers patrolled the other. We stopped on a sandy spot on the shore to take a break. The sand was soft under foot, but the sun felt cool as the clouds came and went. A series of blacker clouds were approaching, and soon we'd be back in the misty rain of May.

It wouldn't be long before we'd be near the top of one of the worst rapids of the trip, Rymes' Pitch. It was a mean place of large, sharp rocks, no clear channel, and several steep drops that would take more than luck to survive. A number of river drivers had drowned there.

Alone
Chapter 4

Earlier that same afternoon and several miles downriver while we were carrying our gear around Nesourdnahunk Falls, eight river drivers sat around the lunch fire at the eddy just above Rymes' Pitch. The coffee had finished brewing, and the beans and brown bread were warmed up. It had been misting all day. The smell of dampness and the chill of the air made for a tough time to be working outside even though it was the first of May.

"We need more men to help us free that jam," said Al Kennedy, the crew boss, carefully rolling a fresh smoke from a can of Prince Albert tobacco. "There's a crew to be had down to Nicatou, below Fowler's." Kennedy put the can back in his plaid shirt pocket and struck a match on the zipper of his fly. "That would be one more bateau for safety." Kennedy lit his smoke. He was a cautious crew boss, more so than most.

"We can free that jam ourselves," Spencer allowed. "We don't need to hire someone else."

"I'm the boss, Spencer, and I'm the one deciding and doing the hiring," said Kennedy. Spencer dragged a foot in the sand, his caulked boot marking a line. Was it a line he dared Kennedy to cross? "I'm going to get help, and you guys need to wait until I get back. That's the beginning and the end of it, understand?" He stared hard at Spencer who took a red handkerchief from his back pocket, cleared his nose, and stuffed the handkerchief back where it came from. "Then, we'll get that jam freed and have our money floating down river again." The pine logs were worth quite a bit, and the crew was going to share in the sale.

Hiring others to help would give them less to divide. Spencer didn't say anything, but he glowered at Kennedy, and then he turned away.

Kennedy left for Nicatou and wouldn't be back for another day. *What were they to do*, Spencer wondered. *Just sit there?*

"What do you say, boys? Let's free that jam," Spencer said to the group after Kennedy left.

"Kennedy isn't going to be very happy if we do this," said Sam. "And I'm not so sure it's a good idea with just one boat.

"We're losing money every minute we sit here," warned Spencer. "If we wait until another crew and boat appear, we'll lose even more. They'll have to be paid if they come to help. That money will come out of our own pockets."

"I think we can do it fine," said Henry, the crew's youngest who was spending his first season on the river. Then he hesitated. "Won't that jam haul when we find and cut the key log?" He was barely eighteen, had no experience on the drive, but he was right. The jam would haul if they could find the key log.

"Maybe," Roger said. "But we'll want an escape route. I don't want to be on a pile of logs that are about to tumble end for end over the rapids. Let's give it a try. Three men can stay with the boat on shore and paddle out to get us if they have to. I don't like the idea of losing money any more than you do."

"You can say that again," Sam said. He was expecting the money he would earn from this drive would be enough for a down payment on the farm he had his eye on. This was his last year working on the river.

"Spencer, Henry and I can be the rescue crew since we have the most experience with the bateau."

The rest agreed with nodding heads, and the men headed to the bateau. Their boat could take a crew of eight. Spencer would take the stern, holding a long spruce pole, lowering it into the rapids from the eddy above. Sam would take the bow, using a second pole to keep the boat parallel with the current. Henry would sit in the middle to row upstream, timing the pulls of the oars to ease the strain on Sam in the stern as he leaned on his pole, releasing it only to get another purchase. The four river drivers who would work on freeing up the jam sat on the remaining seats, plain boards holding the bateau's sides in place. One helped Henry row.

Seven river drivers lowered the bateau into the current from the upper eddy. Using poles, oars and river driver skill, they glided safely across the current. When they reached the jam, they landed in a small eddy behind a rock right beside it. Strong current was on one side of them, but it was calm right behind the huge gray boulder they were aiming for.

Four of them would work the jam. River drivers often worked in pairs, two to a log, using a Peavey to roll them. They had to pick the right logs, or the jam could haul, or move suddenly with or without any warning. When the bateau reached the safety of the eddy beside the jam, four men hopped out onto the pile, scrambling to find the key log that was holding everything up. Sometimes, they had to pick around the edges before it all hauled, but once in a while there would be a single log that, if chopped through in just the right place, would suddenly split apart, freeing the rest of the logs while the axman threw the ax and ran for shore as if the devil were chasing him. Sometimes a little dynamite would be used on jams like this one. Tied to a long stick, the dynamite would be placed far into the pile. A long fuse ran to the end of the stick, "heating up" the jam and freeing it. But they had no dynamite. It gave them no comfort knowing that Kennedy had explosives on his list for his return trip with the extra men. This job was going to be all muscle.

It is dangerous work in spite of wearing spiked, or "caulked" boots, ones that gave them a secure footing when drivers ran across the logs, balancing with a pick pole like acrobats running on a wire. One slip, and it's a tough crawl to get back up on a rolling log.

With four men now working to free the jam, the three managing the bateau poled and rowed back to the upstream eddy where they tied up. The mist had thickened. By six, the crew was ready to come off for supper, having freed up several logs that afternoon. The jam was still hung in the middle of the rapid.

The shore crew of three left the coffee pot hanging over the fire and set out from the little eddy above the rapids for the thirty-foot trip to retrieve the four men on the jam. Sam was poling at the bow, Spencer at the stern, and Henry again at the oars.

"Keep the boat straight," warned Spencer. Sam had let the bow swing too far out, but he brought it back, parallel to the current the next time he set the pole. Moving the bateau into the current, they took the same route across. The plan was to eddy out next to the big gray boulder beside the jam just like before. The men would jump in the boat by the boulder, man the second set of oars and they'd pole and row back up to the eddy. This wasn't a difficult maneuver for experienced river drivers as long as nothing broke.

Just after they left the safety of shore, Spencer's pole snapped in half. Henry couldn't keep the bow straight in the strong current with the oars, and Sam couldn't straighten the boat by himself from the bow. The bateau swung sideways into the maw of the pitch.

The drivers on the jam could only watch the three men struggle with the current. In a moment all three in the boat were thrown into the whitewater, their bateau tumbling end for end. The men on the jam were helpless to do anything about it. Spencer was crushed against a rock by the end of a giant pine log and then he sank out of sight. He didn't come up again. Henry disappeared in a huge souse hole where the strong current poured over a rock with a sharp face. His body would never be found. They last saw Sam holding on to the narrow black-tarred bottom of the overturned bateau, the fast current spinning him around the corner and out of sight.

Their rescue was now up to Sam. If Sam didn't make it, no one else knew where the men were until Kennedy returned the next day with the extra crew to run a safety boat. Maybe the stranded river drivers could last until then, but the water had begun to rise. It must have been the rain from an earlier thundershower just reaching this point in the river. Maybe another gate was opened. The reason didn't matter because the rising water would soon float away those very logs that were now the only refuge from the wild whitewater pushing against the jam. And what would they do if the logs did haul? The only other option was to jump in. And then drown in the darkness amidst the rolling pine logs.

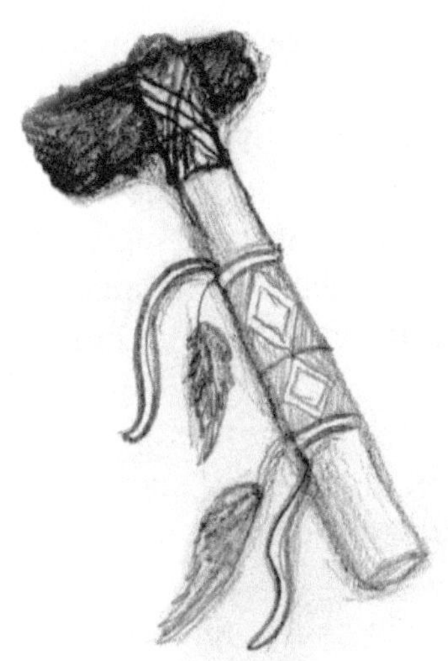

Sam's Ride
Chapter 5

Sam could barely hold on to the bateau's bottom, a narrow plank freshly coated with tar that was as smooth as glass in the icy cold water. His legs dangled down into the current, dragging over the riverbed as his arms stretched to hold on to the slippery hull. There wasn't much to hold on to. When the boat hit a large rock, it threw Spencer over the bateau to the other side. As he slid down the side of the bateau, his hand clawing at the creosoted and tarred wood, the boat spun around and hit another rock, larger than before. A board on his side of the boat split open just in time for Sam's fingers to slide into and grab tight. He felt relieved; that feeling didn't last for long.

The boat spun again, crashing against more rocks. The gap in the split board closed, trapping his fingers. Sam wasn't grabbing the boat anymore. The boat had grabbed him. Down the rapids they went, spinning around, banging off rocks, bouncing Sam about like a bucking bronco desperate to rid itself of its rider, then dragging him over boulder after boulder. First, he was before the upturned bateau, being pushed onto rocks. Then he was dragged behind it, abrading his legs over more rocks. It was a good thing that his fingers were too cold to feel much.

The four river drivers hanging out on the jam had seen none of this since Sam was now well below them and far around the river's bend. It could be a long, drizzly night to sit beside a rising river, praying that the logs didn't haul before someone came to help.

Sam and his bateau spun around once more, and this time, in the middle of Island Falls Pitch, it smashed itself on another log jam, thankfully releasing his fingers and giving Sam his freedom. Immediately after his release, he grabbed one of the logs with his good hand and swung himself over the top. There was no rest for him there. When he stood up, his spiked boots grabbing on to the top of the logs, the entire jam began to haul. All the logs seemed to be moving at the same time, but at different angles. Some had started to roll. Others were sticking straight up in the air. He had maybe three seconds to get to shore before falling between the moving logs.

Sam ran across the jam like a crazed squirrel. Just as the logs were almost too far apart to jump from one to the next, Sam took a last giant leap to shore, just before Grand Pitch, a twenty-foot drop he wouldn't have survived. After he landed in the water next to the riverbank, he cradled his mangled hand, wincing from the rising pain, and dropped onto a boulder in the misty early evening in his wet clothes.

He guessed he was two miles below his buddies left stranded in the middle of Rymes' Pitch. John Fowler's farm and landing would be less than two miles away. There was a well-used logging road that ran from Fowler's to the eddy above Rymes' Pitch. He knew he could do nothing for the men if he went back, but he knew where he could find help. He started for Fowler's farm.

Sam walked down a well-worn trail to the bottom of Grand Pitch where he thought he might find a boat left by other river drivers on their way by. There, tucked away by a big pine, was an overturned rowboat. He found oars and a long pole stored underneath. He had to remember to return the boat; the river men who had left it might need it. Sam rowed through Shad Pond, still on the river, and then poled the boat up Millinocket Stream. Sometimes his hand felt like it was on fire. Once, he almost gave up when the pole slipped off a rock, and he banged his injured hand on the gunwale. The distance from Rymes' Pitch wasn't more than a few miles. Sam felt like it was more like a hundred.

Fowler's Landing was just ahead. Sam got out of the boat, lashing it to an alder, and rushed to the house across the field. Every step he took was filled with pain. When Mrs. Fowler answered the knock at this late hour, she was surprised to see a nearly drowned man, dripping on the threshold, cradling his right arm. His mangled hand was bleeding, fingers not quite as straight as fingers should be.

"Oh, my!" Mrs. Fowler cried. "Mary, come here quick!" She turned back to Sam, placing her hand on his shoulder for encouragement, "Come in you poor man." And in he came, squishing in his caulked boots.

"My boots, ma'am," Sam said, "They'll mark up your floor." And they would leave the floor full of tiny nail prints, turning the boards into wormwood.

"Don't worry about that, you're not the first one to stomp his spiked boots into my kitchen floor" she said, turning away from him but not letting go of his arm as she ushered him through the doorway. She cried out, "Susan! Go get your father now!" Mrs. Fowler turned back to Sam and pointed to a straight-backed chair. "Here, sit right here and let's look at that hand." Mary put a blanket around his shoulders.

When the carry manager, John Fowler came into the room following Susan, he saw some man Mrs. Fowler and her oldest daughter, Mary were tending to. Sam's hand had been so cold, he felt hardly a thing as the wounds were cleaned of boat splinters and a few stitches taken.

"What's going on?" asked Mr. Fowler.

"There's a crew of four men stranded on Rymes' Pitch," Sam told him. "Three of us were on our way out in the bateau to get them when the pole snapped, and we went down the pitch."

"Where are the other two?" Mr. Fowler asked.

"I don't know," Sam said, his voice cracking. "They might have made it, but I don't know. Henry is just a kid, his first time driving. God, I hope he made it to shore." His shoulders were still trembling, more from being upset than from the cold water.

Carefully wrapped in white gauze, fingers splinted, his arm was now supported in a home-made sling. As soon as they were done, another daughter put a plate of food and a cup of hot coffee in front of him.

"I can't stay and eat, ma'am," Sam said. "I have to get back to help my friends. They must think I've forgotten them."

"You need to get your strength up. John will need some help with the rescue," Mrs. Fowler replied sternly, "and you need to be in good enough shape to help him."

"Yes, Ma'am," Sam replied.

"Mary, Susan, come help your mother and me get the Maynard in the wagon." Mr. Fowler left for the barn, his daughters and wife following close behind. Soon they had the bateau in the wagon, oars, rope and poles. Sam finished his supper and joined them outside. Mr. Fowler hitched up the oxen and followed his children, flitting ahead like fireflies lighting the way to Rymes' Pitch.

Rymes' Pitch
Chapter 6

Abby and I unloaded everything and pulled the canoe well on shore just above Rymes' Pitch, a nasty part of the river that snagged more logs than the Heaters, two narrow passages in Ripogenus Gorge. It was nearly dark when we pulled into a little eddy well above the rapid. We were clearly focused on getting to the little beach, not taking any chances with drifting into the whitewater just below us. We had to carry our gear around the whitewater and then come back for the canoe. The path started out easy enough, but it soon wandered over and between large gray rocks. A wheelbarrow wouldn't have worked if we had one. Nor would a travois, a simple drag using two thin spruce poles and a little black spruce root to bind them. I was looking forward to pitching the tent beside the eddy below the falls and getting something to eat. It was beginning to get dark. We carried our gear into a clearing beside the falls.

"Looks like someone's been staying here," I said. Campsites could be found at most of the rapids where canoes, bateaux and gear had to be carried around. I could see some crates of food, a coffee pot hanging from a pole across the fire pit, and a couple of pack baskets. "There are a lot of hot coals here. Coffee's still warm. I'm surprised it was left like this. Where are the river drivers?"

"Do you hear something?" Abby shouted, putting down her pack basket. We were beside the most turbulent part of the rapids, and the roar was pretty loud. I could see one clear tongue of water pouring over a ledge drop right beside us.

"Nope," I shouted back. "Just the rapids. Why?" The pack basket's straps were starting to cut into my shoulders, so I took the opportunity to shrug off the weight to the ground.

"I don't know, I thought…wait, there it is again."

"I just heard something, too. It's coming from the river," I said. "I don't see anything through the fog."

We shouted back. There was no reply. We shouldered our packs again and finished the first trip of the carry. We would have to make several more to move all our gear. It was a nice place to camp with a sandy beach and a nice breeze to keep the skeeters away. When we got to the shore, we looked around and again heard a cry for help.

This time we walked to the shore. The mist was clearing away. There, in the middle of the river, we saw four men sat on the very top of a huge logjam. Where was their boat and shore crew? There was no one around to get them off. If that jam moved, they were done for.

"What are they doing out there? Where's their safety crew?" They were shouting at us, but we couldn't make out the words; the roar of the pulsing rapids drowned them out.

"Don't know. They're not having any fun by the looks. Especially since the water is rising." Abby could be annoyingly matter-of-fact.

"We should try to help them, but first we'd better get our stuff to higher ground or we'll be in trouble, too. This river can rise with little warning," I said. "Let's see if we can find some rope." Daylight was beginning to fade as the sun dropped behind the mountains.

We didn't find anything. No bateaux. No rope. We shouted together to hang tight and we'd find someone to help. We had to find the nearest farm.

"There's the path to Fowler's Farm," Abby said. "It's the closest one." We started along the path when we saw yellow lights coming toward us.

Holding birch bark torches, two of John Fowler's children were skipping along in the mist of the falls. Behind them was an ox cart that carried a Maynard, a high-sided bateau. A man walked behind the cart, his bandaged hand supported by a sling and bound across his chest.

In the cart were several hanks of heavy rope, block and tackle, and several rollers for getting the Maynard down to the water. Long poles, Peaveys and axes were lashed to the sides. When the wagon passed by, I could see a box of kindling, fire starting moss and birch bark for more torches and illuminating fires on the shore. Very soon, it would be pitch black on this cold, wet May night while four men held on to a pile of logs that was about to haul and roll them over.

Abby and I were surprised to see a rescue team led by children. John Fowler and an injured man had arrived to rescue the river drivers stranded on the log jam in the middle of the rapids.

"Come help unload the boat," John shouted to us. He backed the cart to the little beach. Two children stood by, holding their torches so we could see what we were doing. The third was busy lighting fires along the shore to illuminate the rapids. Over the sound of the river, we could hear the men cheering.

"We'll take this side," said Abby, grabbing onto the rope that hung out the back of the ox powered wagon. The Maynard was heavy, and the four of us had to keep it from falling to the ground.

"Easy now," John directed. "We can't let this drop." We let the boat down to the ground.

"I'll get the rollers," I said, and jumped into the wagon to hand them out. Abby placed them under the boat. John and the other man lifted it by the side. Then, bit by bit, the three of us dragged the boat on the rollers toward the little beach. John began loading the Maynard with ropes, poles, and oars.

By now there were four fires the children started, lighting up the sky just enough to chase the darkness away. The orange and red colored flames reflected into the misty air, projecting a rosy glow on the jam, the glistening wet ledges, the men, and the Maynard bateau we were preparing for the rescue attempt.

"I'm taking the stern," John said. "Aren't you Caleb King's boy?" He looked at me.

"Charlie King," I replied.

"And you?" he looked at Abby.

"Abby Ross."

"Not Jim's daughter?" he asked in amazement.

"'Fraid so," she said with a smile. Her father's reputation as a competent drive boss was well known. He directed the crews and made the decisions about which squirt dam to release and when. If water releases were not coordinated, an entire winter's work could be hung up and lost.

"Okay, then Charlie, you take the bow and steady it with the pole. Abby can help Sam row. He needs only one arm for that. He can sit on his good side." We rolled the bateaux into the water. I stood and braced my legs behind the front seat with a torch lashed to the bow.

Sam was in the middle beside Abby. John took the stern seat, his pole in hand. Fog wrapped around us at times, making it hard to see the men not fifty feet away.

"Push out," ordered John and we gently pushed out into the river, keeping the boat headed slightly into the current to keep it from swinging uncontrollably down river. John's pole and our rowing kept the boat from going down the rapids. We could control just how fast we slid across the current. My job was to grab just a little angle while John kept the bateau from slipping too far down river, and Abby and Sam rowed. We dropped into a small eddy just below the jam. When John jammed his pole behind two rocks to hold us in place, I did the same from the bow.

The men were already climbing down the log pile to meet us. The water had risen quite a bit, and already some logs were groaning. Once, we heard a loud "snap" from the middle of the pile of logs, but nothing seemed to happen. Two men were now climbing down into the boat with the third right behind. The three of them settled into the Maynard, and two relieved Sam from his painful chore.

"My foot's stuck!" the fourth man hollered out, still halfway down to the boat. There was another "snap" from the log pile, but this one was much louder. If the rising water didn't float these logs off the rocks, it seemed that the sheer weight of the jam would snap enough logs for it to haul on its own.

"I'll go help him," Abby said, dropping her oars. She was out of the boat, climbing up the pile to the stranded driver before anyone could object. There were no spikes in her boots. My heart was in my throat watching her clamber up the pile to the trapped driver.

"She's like a cat," I said, watching her scramble up to help free his foot.

"I hope she has nine lives, because that jam is about to haul," said John, "and we have to leave right now, or we'll get caught in it! Push the bow out!"

Abby reached the remaining river driver, and she freed his foot just as the logs below them were starting to move.

"Abby, jump now!" I shouted. She was going to be crushed by the logs if she stayed there another second. Both jumped, sliding over the moving logs like frantic otters, jumping forward and then tumbling into the boat while the rescued men rowed, John poled, and I steered us toward the beach above Rymes' Pitch. Just as we left the eddy beside the jam, the entire pile of logs let go with loud screeches and grinding noises. Logs were tumbling like pine needles shaken off a bedroll. We got across the current to safety, the entire jam clearing free from the rocky pitch. Between the children holding torches and the small campfires they had lit along the shore, we were able to see our way back to the beach. We worked as a team, two rescued men at the oars doubling the rowing power. They would take a big stroke ahead while John and I set our poles to hold the boat from slipping back in the current. Stroke, pole set, stroke, we made it across in no time at all.

One of the children grabbed the bow when we reached the sandy beach. The rescued men helped us unload the gear and hoist the Maynard back into the wagon. We then loaded the gear John had brought into the bateau along with all the gear and supplies the river drivers had. For a moment, the rescued men waited at the side of the wagon.

"What about Henry and Spencer?" Sam asked.

"I think the river got them," one of the drivers said. "I watched Henry disappear in the big souse-hole. He never came up. If he did, we never saw it."

"A big log nailed Spencer up against that big rock just below the jam," said Roger. I saw it hit him pretty hard in the small of his back. I don't think he made it either." He paused a moment and looked down at his feet. "We'll see more than one pair of boots hanging from a tree by the end of the drive." It was the custom to lace together the caulked boots worn by a drowned driver and hang them on a tree where his body was recovered. That could take all summer, and the body might not be found at all, instead resting on the river bottom under a heavy pine log until the river next flooded and the body flushed out.

The rescued men went with John to the farm where they'd wait for Kennedy's return, riding in the bateau that had saved their lives. The children lit the way just like before. Abby and I made camp beside the carry. The lights faded as the oxen pulled the heavy load back to the farm.

"What were you trying to do?" I asked her after our baked bean dinner. "You could have been hurt." I reached out for her hand. "I couldn't stand it if something bad happened to you." I found myself teetering between fear for her safety and anger about what she did. I had just lost Mother. I couldn't stand to lose Abby, too. Abby seemed to act without thinking. I didn't expect her response.

"And you could have been hurt, too, Charlie. Anyone could have been. I was closest to help. It all worked out." She seemed rather matter-of-fact, and I've learned not to get in her way. We were exhausted, and even though I had been really scared for her safety, I was really proud of how she handled herself.

It wasn't long before we fell asleep. The mist had disappeared, and we could see the stars through the opening in the tent, an army canvas draped over a rope. There were no black bears in my dreams that night, just a pair of black wings coming for me, Ki'kwa'jenu's coal-red eyes glowing in the dark.

We woke to a clear, calm morning on the little beach above Rymes' Pitch. We packed up the tent, and Abby went looking for some wild mint for her tea. By the time she returned, I had a fire going and oatmeal cooking. I had made some coffee, but Abby preferred tea, so an extra pot was on the fire for hot water.

"Do you think we'll be there by this afternoon?" I asked.

She thought a minute. "Nicatou isn't that far away now. If we make good time to Debsconeag, we'll be at Grandmother Molly's before sunset.

"I'm glad we brought the rifle," I said, finishing my coffee. I had seen some bear scat on my trip to the bushes and back. "It's a good deterrent when it comes to bears."

"And other varmints," Abby added. "There were times I was glad my father carried a pistol with him on our trips cruising timber, especially when we'd meet some trappers. Just having it on his hip where it could be seen was enough to keep them from bothering us."

"Did they ever bother you?"

"Once or twice, but Father was quick to recognize leering looks. All he had to do was rest his hand on the pistol grip, and they got the idea pretty fast."

We packed up the rest of our gear, loaded the canoe, and began paddling the deadwater to the next carrying place just above Grand

Pitch. The sun felt warm on my face after a cold, misty night on the riverbank. I wasn't looking forward to lugging our gear and the canoe down the carry trail that ran beside Grand Pitch, the longest set of rapids we had to portage, but I had no choice. An hour later, we were loaded up again and on our way over much calmer water.

The East Branch flowed into the West Branch at Nicatou. We turned into it and paddled just a little way up the tributary. "We're almost there," Abby said from the back of the canoe. "See that landing just ahead?" Some smoke was rising through the trees farther up the island. Someone had a campfire.

"I can see some smoke. Is that the village where Grandmother Molly lives?" I asked.

"It's been a while," she replied. "But I'm pretty sure that's the place."

We paddled across the slight current to the landing. There, we could see several other canoes turned over beside a little path leading away from the riverbank. It looked like some had been there for a while, covered with maple leaves from more than a few fall seasons. After we leaned our canoe against a birch tree, we grabbed our packs and followed the path to a small clearing surrounded by tents, shacks, and a couple of log cabins. We stepped over more bear scat. Slung over my shoulder, the rifle was comforting.

Children ran about the yard, laughing and chasing after a boy in an apparent game of tag. A moose hung from a game pole, and some chickens pecked here and there. Small garden plots ringed the clearing. In another month there would be rows and rows of corn planted with peas, beans and squash all using the corn stalk to climb on. A tall, carved totem pole with brightly painted features and adorned with moose and deer antlers was off to one side. We could hear the fat from the critter on the spit hissing on the hot coals of the fire as we approached. Their dinner smelled really good.

Several adults were gathered around the fire pit in the center of the clearing. Plaid flannel shirts were most popular with both men and women standing there. We didn't find out until later why they seemed so serious. When they saw us, they stopped talking and stared at two strangers from another culture invading their space. One man who had been sitting on a log poking the fire, looked our way, stood up and approached us.

"Can I help you?" he asked politely. His black hair hung down his chest in long braids decorated with colored yarns.

"We're looking for my grandmother, Molly Fairweather," Abby replied. He studied us for a moment, paying special attention to Abby.

"You mean 'Awasosqua'," he said.

"That's right," Abby asked. Our lessons in the old language with Olive were paying off. When meeting strangers coming into their village, speaking in the old language seemed a declaration of independence as if to say, "This is our place. You are foreigners and don't belong."

"I can see Awasosqua in your face; you look just like her," he said to Abby, pointing to a path that left the clearing just ahead. "Follow that path and you'll come right to her door. Shout at the camp from the edge of the clearing when you see it," he suggested, "She has been a little busy lately helping the sick."

Abby thanked him, and we were on our way.

"Why would your grandmother be helping the sick?" I asked. "Is she a nurse?"

"I don't know," Abby said. "She does know about medicinal plants I remember. There don't seem to be too many people around. I was expecting to see more." We met no one along the path.

"Maybe they're out hunting or fishing," I said. The trip to meet her grandmother and to learn about the amulet was making me feel a little anxious. That 'Awasosqua' meant 'mother bear' was no comfort. Dreams of bears, knowing bears had been visiting campsites, stories of leering trappers, men marooned in the middle of the river were all taking its toll on any serenity I had before we left home. I liked things easy; this trip had been far from it.

The path to Molly's home was wide enough for a small cart and horse. Sap season had passed, the red maples were beginning to leaf out, and some dandelions were poking through last fall's leaves along our way. I could see a canopy of flowering cherry branches arching over the path while a few gray squirrels hunted for left-over nuts, hungry after a long, frozen winter.

Her house wasn't a shanty or a shack. She lived in a neat cabin with a cedar shake roof, a screened-in covered porch that ran around three sides, and several small sheds and what looked like a bunk house out back. I could see a field stone chimney angling through the roof with a thin wisp of white smoke drifting away from it. Next to the cabin was a small shed where she kept her firewood out of the snow and rain. There was a neat row of split cherry, ash and oak for those colder spring days. Kindling and wood for the cook stove were piled on the back porch out of the weather. Blood and feathers on a chopping block nearby told me that chickens had taken their last breaths there.

"Hello the camp," Abby shouted. It was a custom to announce oneself when approaching a residence in the north woods. Startling a resident who might have a loaded shotgun beside the door wasn't a safe thing to do. Grandmother Molly was nowhere to be seen. There was no answer to Abby's call.

Abby and I walked around the back and found another small building with a little porch, a boardwalk connecting one cabin door to the other. Hanging from the rafters along the front porch were dozens of dream catchers and feathers. A deer hide was stretched out in a frame. Several skulls had been nailed to one of the posts. Two large ones were at the top of the post with smaller skulls in descending size just below.

"I wonder what those skulls come from?" I mused aloud.

"The big one is from a very angry bear I killed years ago," came the reply from behind us. We turned around to see a small woman wearing a deerskin cape over a skirt, decorated leggings, and a peaked hood that looked like it had been made from birch bark with feathers and tufts of animal fur at the top.

"She nearly got me, that one she did." She looked at Abby. "I miss your mother so much," she said. "She had the same red hair and dark brown eyes. You look so much like her." Molly reached out her arms, and she pulled Abby into a warm embrace. Abby hugged her back and tilted her head to me.

"This is Charlie," she said. "His grandmother was a Beothuk, too." With their dark, almond shaped eyes, high cheekbones and oval faces, Abby and Molly looked like sisters.

When Molly reached out her hand and took mine, my skin began to tingle. I had never felt that before. The tingling stopped when we disconnected, and I wondered what that meant.

"Come inside. I am glad you have come. We will have tea, and you will tell me about your journey."

Molly led Abby by the hand over the boardwalk toward the cabin's back door while I followed. She removed her peaked hat and placed it on a shelf just inside the back door.

Her cabin was crammed. More dream catchers hung from the ceiling joists. Clay jars of different sizes lined rows of shelves. There were unique decorations on each, and each was covered by thin deerskin, a band of string securing it to the jar. I didn't want to seem nosy, so I didn't ask what was in them. Abby could tell me later, I thought. There were plant stalks of every description, ends bound with string, hanging wherever there was room to set another nail. Molly noticed what I was studying.

"The jars and the plants are the herbs I use for healing the sick. Some are for our ceremonies," she said. Molly pointed to a larger jar. "That one has the red ochre we use for special ceremonies." The otherwise clear glass jar was full of red chunks and powder of ferric oxide. If you got it on your skin, it turned reddish orange and took a long time to wash away. The smell of mint mingled with wood smoke gave a homey aroma to the cabin.

Totems hung on the walls beside framed photos of earlier tribal elders, and there were a few shelves of what looked like carved wooden statues a few inches high. Some totems were painted; others were plain. Several strings of bear claws hung from wooden pegs fastened to the beams above the table.

She motioned to the table for us to sit, and then brought out three cups. Opening one of the jars on the countertop near her sink, she measured a spoonful of ground teaberry leaves for each cup and poured in water that had been heating on her wood cook stove. She refilled the teapot with water from the pitcher pump beside the slate sink.

"I can't sit for long," Molly said. "I have some medicine to make."

"What's wrong?" Abby asked. Molly returned to the table and slowly took her chair.

"There is sickness here. It has spread quickly throughout the village. No doctor or hospital can help them One has already died here, and two have died at the hospital in Bangor. Without the right medicine, others will, too. The illness is far beyond their powers to heal. Victims first lose their sense of taste and smell. Many have a sore throat. Soon there's a headache and high fever with a nasty cough. Every breath is filled with pain. The illness can last for two weeks. Most of my patients are elderly.

"How many are sick?" I asked.

"Nearly thirty now, probably half the village. They're not coming into our little make-shift hospital as fast as two days ago when eight walked in the same afternoon," Molly described.

"Let us know if there's anything we can do to help," offered Abby.

"I will. Our village is having a small celebration tonight in the middle of all this sickness," she said. "You are welcome to join us." Having a meal other than beans or oatmeal sounded great.

"Is there a special occasion?" Abby asked.

"Because we begin our planting tomorrow, we always have a feast the night before to show our thanks to the Great Spirit." Molly set the cups in front of us. "Here's some milk," she offered, placing a small can of evaporated milk on the table. Broken off match sticks plugged the two holes in the top of the can. "Sugar is in the jar." She sat down and looked outside. She seemed preoccupied, concerned possibly, but not anxious.

"Tell me about your trip," Molly said. Abby told her about the near miss when we pulled to the river's edge above the falls. Then she went into the details of the rescue at Rymes' Pitch.

"The Fowlers are good people," Molly said. "They helped me when I first arrived in this country."

"I thought you had always lived here," Abby said.

The Amulet
Chapter 8

We were sitting at Grandmother Molly's kitchen table having tea. Molly had been talking about the places she had lived. She talked about her family tree, but her next story was nearly too fantastic to believe.

"I come from an earlier time. There was still a remnant of a glacier between Tumbledown and Owl's Peak." Molly's face looked like it had been chiseled from rock. She studied our faces, taking note of our reaction to such an implausible statement.

"What?" Abby said, her brow furrowed above a stony stare.

"That can't be possible," I added. "There haven't been glaciers here for thousands of years!" This woman was definitely a crazy lady, tribal leader or not. I thought we should probably say our good-byes and head home while we could. Who knew what she would do?

Grandmother Molly waited a moment longer to let the thought sink in. "Do you remember seeing this?" she asked, pulling out a golden, translucent amulet from under her shirt. The amulet looked perfectly round and had some engravings around the outer edge. There was a small hole at the top for the deerskin lace that kept it around her neck. She took it off and handed it to Abby.

"I do," Abby answered. "I remember seeing you wear it when I was a little girl. It's actually what got me thinking about coming to see you."

"Hiram told us the story about its creation and how Katahdin found it," I said.

"This amulet was given to me by my father, a great shaman of our Neptune clan." Molly paused again. "The clan was in trouble. A stranger had come. I had just turned sixteen when a strange man seemed to walk out of the shadows. No one had ever seen him before. He spoke with an annoying rasp as if a raven were speaking."

"Wasn't it hard to understand what he said?" Abby asked.

"We could understand okay, but he was really annoying to listen to," Molly explained. "He was taller than most of us with black raven feathers in his headband. He wore hawk's talons on a necklace around his neck. We called him Blackfeather. Soon after he appeared, Blackfeather helped us find game. He seemed to know where the moose and deer were grazing. It was as if he could see everything from high up in the tallest tree."

"The clan must have loved him for that. Hunting is tough in the best of times," I said. I found myself going along to be polite, but also because of Grandmother Molly's story telling. She was so entrancing.

"Finding game wasn't Blackfeather's only contribution," Molly said. "He could locate a canoe that had drifted away from the shore, and when two children ignored their parents' warnings about the Nodumkanwet that lived in the swamp and went missing, he was able to send the search party right to the quicksand they were mired in. It was just in time, too."

"That's amazing. How was he able to do it?" I asked. I was having a hard time believing what she said, but I played along to see what would come next.

"No one knew, but as time passed there were suspicions. People became afraid of his temper. One day," Grandmother Molly said, "He was angered when he didn't get his own way, and a strong wind suddenly arose that brought down a lot of trees next to the village. Several thought he could summon the north wind, Kabibonokka." You might remember that I had a similar relationship with Sowanakik, the south wind. When I was angry or those close to me were in danger, the south wind would suddenly rise to a gale. Some of Molly's story could have been about me.

Molly paused and sipped from her mug. "Blackfeather wanted a wife," she went on, "and he asked Little Otter Feet. *Wne kikw* rebuffed him publicly, probably thinking that doing so would keep him away from her. "The next day, she was missing. Her family could not find her anywhere. My father sent out search parties, but nothing was ever found except for evidence of a huge wind that had uprooted some trees and a giant black feather. Most thought that Ki'kwa'jenu had taken her."

"Would the Nighthawk do that?" I asked.

"Ki'kwa'jenu was often blamed for disappearances," Molly replied and continued her story. "Blackfeather was asked if he could find her the way he saw moose and deer. He said he saw moose grazing on pond lilies by Ripogenus Mountain, but he didn't see anything of Little Otter Feet."

"That must have been hard to lose someone that way but not know what happened," Abby said.

"She was never found. The same thing happened again a month later," Grandmother Molly said. "Blackfeather knew exactly where the game was, and the clan prospered. Then Blackfeather approached Little Raccoon, the daughter of a very talented arrowhead flaker. When Little Azeban rejected him in front of her friends, he went to the lodge he had just built and did not join in the evening's meal. The next morning, Little Azeban was nowhere to be found. Everyone looked for her. Near the village, the searchers were blocked by a tangle of trees. It looked like a tornado had touched down, and again there was one large Nighthawk feather, but no Little Azeban. Blackfeather was asked, and again he said he could see elk grazing on the mesa and mountain goats on Grandfather Mountain, but no Little Azeban."

"Wasn't anyone getting suspicious of Blackfeather?" Abby asked. "I mean, it's pretty clear to me that he was somehow involved."

"Blackfeather made a lot of friends since he appeared. Several were always in his company, telling him how wonderful he was, and he was good to them in return. They had the best of the hunts because Blackfeather would share some hunting opportunities that he kept from the rest of the clan. Many were reluctant to point a finger at such an asset. They were afraid they might need food." Molly stood up. "I have to stretch these old bones," she complained, and walked over to her stove to refill her mug for more tea. "You want more?" she asked us.

"I'm fine," I said.

"I'd like some more," said Abby. Molly filled her mug and sat in the rocker beside the table. "What happened to Blackfeather?"

Molly looked into her mug a moment, and as she raised her eyes to ours, I had an uncomfortable premonition that somehow, I was going to meet this guy. I could feel it in my tightening chest. He was going to jump out of one of my dreams or something just like the Nighthawk.

"My father, Gray Wolf, told me that there was some connection between Blackfeather, Ki'kwa'jenu and Kabibonokka, but he wasn't sure what it was. Then Little Pezo went missing a few days after she refused Blackfeather's request for marriage."

"That's the third one!" Abby cried. "Did the clan still think he was innocent?"

"Some did, and some didn't. It was about fifty-fifty," Molly explained. "When the search parties headed out, again Blackfeather was asked if he could see her like the elk, deer and moose, but he said he could not. A giant feather from Ki'kwa'jenu was discovered driven through the roots of an upturned giant pine. A few days before I left, young Moosis, one of my cousins, followed Blackfeather through the woods. Blackfeather was pretty angry about something, and seemed to bring up a strong north wind, almost as if he had summoned Kabibonokka. Poor Moosis was so scared, he ran home, hearing giant wings flapping behind him. Blackfeather is a good one to stay away from."

"Did they ever find the missing girls?" I asked.

"No, nothing was ever found, neither a moccasin nor a piece of bone." Molly said and paused. "And then, a month or so later, Blackfeather asked me to marry him."

"Oh no!" said Abby. "What happened?"

"Gray Wolf was convinced that I should leave the village. Three had disappeared, and I could be next. My father gave me this amulet to protect me." She pointed to the golden yellow talisman. "This amulet is very powerful, different from other forces in the spirit world. The person who wears it can travel through many centuries."

Abby looked again at the object in her hand, looked at me, and started to hand it back when Grandmother Molly raised her hand for Abby to stop.

"There is much responsibility for the person who possesses it," she said. "There are rituals that, when performed correctly, will take you back and forth between many generations."

"You're not saying *you're* thirty-five hundred years old?" Abby asked.

Molly laughed. "No, Abby. I turned seventy-five last month. I came here from a time very long ago, and for a very good reason, protection from Blackfeather."

Always the practical one, Abby asked, "How does it work?" She examined the amulet in her hand, turning it over and over.

Grandmother Molly sure could tell a tall tale, I thought.

"First, there has to be a good reason to travel," Molly warned, "or the spirits won't listen, and the travelers might not end up where they intended to be."

I had so many questions, but I thought better of asking any. It wouldn't have made a difference as I thought we were in the cabin of a nut case, and we'd better say good-bye and get home. This trip was a waste of time.

Molly looked out the window a moment before continuing. It seemed that the story was not an easy one for her to tell. "He was afraid I would also disappear, so he sent me away. It was so hard for me to leave. It was the last thing I wanted to do." Molly wiped her eyes. "He gave the amulet to me, taught me how to use it in the Skull Cave and warned me that I should take it away and never return," Molly continued, her eyes beginning to water.

"But why here?" Abby asked.

"Don't you mean 'Why *now*?'" Molly smiled, wiping her eyes. "I know how this must sound to you. We are in almost the same physical place now; the old village site is just beyond those trees."

"Why *this* time, then?" Abby asked again.

"There are words to go with the amulet," Molly said. "Some turn the clock's hand one way just so far, and others turn it backwards."

"But that's thirty-five centuries!" I exclaimed. "Why not one or two? Wouldn't that have done the same thing?"

"I made a mistake in the ritual," she replied. "Father wanted me to be far enough away so that few memories of our time would survive, and no one would care who I was, so we planned for me to travel a generation away. But I sent myself much farther away than either of us intended, and I didn't dare go back to the cave to repeat the ritual. I was afraid that I would meet up with Blackfeather and meet the same fate as the others."

"You have to go back to Skull Cave to start over?" Abby asked.

"Yes, if something goes wrong. Going back to the cavern is the only way to reset the clock," Grandmother Molly said.

It was a lot to take in. I thought it would be best to listen instead of question, even better, take a long walk - but I stayed. There was something compelling about Molly's story and I wanted to hear more.

"When you came here," Abby asked, "you couldn't have known anyone. The language must have been so different! How were you able to fit in that many years later?" I had to wonder what it would be like to leave everyone you know and start over in a different place….and time.

"To those living here, it looked like I simply walked out of the woods one day. Some things had changed, of course, but people here wore the same traditional clothing that I did. What I wore simply looked like an older style. No one asked questions. True, the language was a little different, but many basic words were just the same. I could make myself understood. The more I spoke, the more I showed people how different I was. It was as if I had a different accent that was hard to understand. People here accepted me for who I was. A family took me in, and I became a member of this Beothuk clan. They realized how skilled I was at locating medicinal plants. That was my contribution." Molly paused a moment while she scanned the shelves with the clay jars. "That is my strength," she said, looking at the jars. "I kept the amulet a secret, and I never returned home." She looked out the window for a moment. Then she turned to us.

"I had a young sister in the old times. Her name was Nolka or Running Deer. After I left, Nolka could have been Blackfeather's choice for a wife, whether or not she wanted him, but Nolka was too young, just twelve or thirteen summers. To protect her, my father gave her a clear crystal pendant. It was the same one that was handed down from father to daughter as long as anyone could remember."

"Why did you get the amulet and Nolka the crystal pendant?" Abby asked.

"Because I was much older. Nolka was not as adventurous as I was," Molly explained. "She would have had a harder time making the adjustments I had to make when I arrived here."

"Boy, I wish I could go back in time," I mused. "I could see my mother again."

"Same here," Abby said. We were quiet for a moment. "You told us about the origin of the amulet," she asked Grandmother Molly. "What about the crystal pendant?"

"Every member of my clan from long ago knew that story by heart. Big Thunder, a Beothuk hunter from the land of many rivers, went to visit the spirit of Pomola. His hunting had gone well, and he wanted to thank Pomola for the game he found. Big Thunder dressed in his finest deer skin and painted his face with red ochre. No one had ever been able to reach Pomola's home in the mountain range where the spirit of Katahdin lived. Fierce winds, rain and snow from the spirit of the north wind, Kabibonokka, had kept all others away, but Big Thunder found himself closer than anyone else had ever been. When Pomola saw him climbing, he sent the fury of the wind down the slopes to push Big Thunder away."

"Did Big Thunder try again?" Abby asked.

"He was not discouraged," Molly replied. "Soon, Big Thunder climbed again toward Alomkik, Pomola's home. But Pomola was not done with him. He sent Kabibonokka down over the boulders, covering Big Thunder with heavy snows. Big Thunder was able to light a small warming fire and heat some bear fat, dripped onto the coals in a tribute to Pomola. When Pomola smelled the bear fat, he descended to Big Thunder.

"'Welcome brother,' Big Thunder said to Pomola.

"'No other Indian has ever called me brother,' Pomola replied. 'Brothers should be together'," she continued.

"Pomola picked up Big Thunder, placed him on his shoulder, and flew away to his home in the mountains. There, wigwams, venison and warming fires gave Big Thunder all he could possibly want. He married Pomola's daughter, Wajo. After a year passed, Big Thunder was allowed to return home with the warning that he was not to marry again.

"But Big Thunder disobeyed and planned to marry a beautiful woman from his earthly tribe. On the eve of the wedding, Big Thunder disappeared during a fierce windstorm. It is thought that Pomola and Kabibonokka were responsible. There was no marriage since there was no longer a groom.

"Pomola's problems were only beginning. His daughter, Wajo, loved Big Thunder. She was distraught that he had disappeared, and she began to look for him. Pomola's anger towards Big Thunder faded when he saw how unhappy Wajo had become. She searched for Big Thunder every chance she had, and one day Wajo's desperation and grief became unbearable. She threw herself into a ravine.

"When Pomola went to look for his daughter, he found a crystal of quartz embedded in the rock. It was the pendant she had always worn. There was no other sign of Wajo. She was gone forever. After removing the crystal from the rock, Pomola howled in grief. His tears made the rivers overflow their banks, and much land was flooded. To make amends to Big Thunder's bride-to-be in the Beothuk village below, he gave the crystal to her. It would allow the holder to summon the Great Spirit for protection from enemies."

"Did his village bride ever find Big Thunder?" Abby asked.

"No, she never did. Big Thunder was gone forever; Pomola saw to that. Those who seek Pomola face the winds, the snow, lightning, hail and rain. No one has ever returned from the journey to Pomola's lodge. The crystal was a powerful symbol that remained with her family and was handed down from father to daughter.”

“The story I’ve heard is that no one dares to climb the mountain for fear of meeting Pomola,” Abby remarked. “How did the crystal pendant protect Nolka?

“Because it had the power of Pomola within it. The person to whom it was given was kept from harm,” Molly explained. “Together, the amulet and the pendant would give the holder much power. Father thought the greater distance the relics were kept apart, the better. He was never comfortable possessing both, and he worried about what could happen if they fell into the wrong hands.”

“Like Blackfeather’s? Why didn’t your father use both to make Blackfeather disappear into the past?” Abby asked.

“My father felt it was too risky. He knew a story about another shaman who tried to use them together to defeat a raiding party from far away. When he did, the story goes, an entire village was destroyed in a windstorm created by Kabeyun, the spirit of all winds. That’s why he kept his possession of the crystal a secret.”

“He sent you away with the amulet to protect you and the tribe?” Abby asked. “I would have been pretty upset.”

Grandmother Molly stared into her mug of tea, and she was quiet for a moment. “I haven’t seen my father for a very long time. It seems like just yesterday I found my way from the village to the cavern in Skull Cave to get away from Blackfeather. There are days when I wish time would move faster. Then maybe my loss would not be as painful.”

I knew what Molly was talking about. We both thought the more time passed after a loss, the more the heart heals, but I haven’t found that to be true when I think of Mother.

“But couldn’t you have gone back?” I asked. “It does work both ways, right?”

“It does, and I could have returned and even visited with him, but it would have been a great risk if I had been found with this,” she answered, pointing to the amulet in Abby’s hands. “And a greater risk if Blackfeather found me.”

“But wouldn’t he be an old man after seventy years have passed?” Abby asked.

“That depends on the time the traveler chooses to return to. If that’s the time I left from, Nolka will still be there, and Gray Wolf should be there, too,” Grandmother Molly said. “But also Blackfeather.”

I thought about going back in time to fix a few things. Mother and Tommy would be alive. I was thinking about what to change, when

Abby saw my attention flag.

"Charlie, you look a little lost," Abby said, calling me back to the present. She seemed to see what I was thinking.

"Oh, sorry," I said. Abby's grandmother seemed so convincing that I found it more difficult not to accept her story. At least I could pretend a little. "It must have been hard to leave everything so suddenly," I said to Molly.

"It was, but I met your grandfather here, and not long after, your mother was born," she said, looking at Abby with a kind smile. Then her smile faded to a serious look as she scanned the pots of medicine along the shelf over our table.

"May I ask you about my grandfather? I don't know anything about him," Abby asked.

"He was a brave hunter, the most handsome one in the village," Molly smiled. "He lost his life on a hunting trip not long after we were married. We weren't together very long. And then I met Hiram."

"Hiram told us he came here to see you; I thought he preferred his own company and his chickens to being with people. Does he visit often?" I asked.

"Why don't you ask him yourself? Look down the path now," Molly said.

I knew who it was the minute I saw a tall figure winding through the garden plots in front of the cabin. With that loping gait and a green, wide brimmed felt hat, it couldn't have been anyone else.

"Get in here, you old coot," Molly admonished him. "We've got company."

Awasosqua
(Mother Bear)
Chapter 9

From where she was sitting, Abby could not see the path Hiram was on, and when she leaned forward to get a better look, Hiram had come up to the porch and was opening the cabin door.

"You look surprised to see me," Hiram said. Abby was nearly speechless. "Hiram?" she asked.

"One and the same," he replied with a little smile.

"I didn't think we'd see you here," Abby said.

"Yeah," I said. "I thought you were going to work on the barn roof at the Inn?"

"Caleb and I had a disagreement about that job," Hiram explained, "so I got done early, and when I went to get my pay, he happened to mention that you two were coming down this way. It's been way too long since I was here last, so I packed some things, hitched a ride with a tow boat coming down for supplies, then a wagon ride, and here I am." Hiram had lived alone, and I always thought he preferred the company of his chickens to people. I knew he left the village from time to time, and now I think I know where he was going.

"Awasosqua and I have been together on and off for what, Molly, nearly sixty years now?"

"About right, Hi," Molly said. "And they've been mostly good ones now you've smartened up. When I first came here, it was difficult being away from my father and sister, especially after my husband died so young, but Hiram took most of the pain away." Molly smiled at Hiram. "He's a good man."

"'Awasosqua' is a strong name," said Abby.

"And she fiercely protects her cubs," Hiram added with a smile. Molly looked out the window where we could see the cooking fires through the trees.

"Nice to see you both," Hiram continued with his greeting. "I hope your trip has gone well."

"There's a lot to tell, Hiram," I said. "It hasn't been an easy one."

"If it's about the men being marooned on Rymes' Pitch, I know all about it," he offered. Kennedy's crew passed by me on my way here, and Sam told me what happened. You two were very brave to have helped in that rescue."

"It's a small world! How's Sam s hand?" I asked.

"He's bandaged up pretty well, and it's very sore he told me, but he will heal. He didn't lose any fingers."

"We don't have much time to reminisce," Molly interrupted. "I was telling about our troubles here, and you need to split wood for the kitchen stove like you promised. I have to finish preparing those plants we collected this morning."

"A man's work is never done at this cabin," he sighed. Hiram walked out the back door, and soon we could hear his ax at work. Molly turned to us. "You've come just in time." She seemed to have trouble getting up to make another mug of tea. I wondered how Molly would be able to take care of herself the coming winter. Lugging water and chopping firewood would be tough tasks for her by herself. Hiram would be a huge help. Maybe now that they were older, they would spend more time together, I hoped.

"I need a certain plant," Molly replied. "If I can find it, I can make a syrup that will cure the sick."

"Just tell us what it looks like, and we'll go searching," Abby said.

"That's the problem," Grandmother Molly said. "It used to grow everywhere around here, but something must have happened over time, and it's no longer growing anywhere around. I know, I look for special plants all the time on hunting and fishing trips, every time I walk through the woods."

"It's probably all the clearcutting the Company has been doing," I suggested. When acres of trees are stripped off the land, not only do the critters who lived there have to find new homes. Plants native to the area don't always survive, silted in streams produce no fish, and the water is not as clear and clean.

"But it does grow where you came from?" asked Abby.

"Yes, and I can tell you where to find it," was the quick reply.

Abby and I looked at each other. While I was wondering what was coming next, Hiram brought in an armful of white birch and dumped it into wood box by the stove.

"Is the only solution to go back using the amulet, and then return with the plant?" Abby was always good at anticipating.

"It is, but that is something Hiram and I cannot do," Molly said. "We are too old to make the trip, and although I might not appear now like I did then, I might still be recognized. It's far too risky for me to return, and my body isn't strong enough to make the trip safely. But you could go. You could fit in. Find Nolka; she will help you. I can show you what the plant looks like. Once gathered, you return with the medicine."

Abby was nodding her head. As hard as it was for me to believe, Awasosqua made some sense, and I found myself nodding, too. I looked at Abby. Then I looked at Molly. Then back again. They were staring at each other as if I weren't even in the room. I decided it would be a great time to excuse myself, step outside and stretch my legs that were far too long for the short chair I had been sitting in.

I left them at the table while I explored the little settlement and thought some more about what we were being asked to do. When I started down the path, I could hear Hiram's ax. I turned around and walked back over the boardwalk and turned to the woodshed. Hiram was working up some white birch for Molly's stove.

"Hey, Charlie!" I heard Hiram say as he brought the ax down, sending four pieces of firewood scattering.

"How'd you know it was me?" I asked. "You never even looked my way!"

"That's because you make more noise than a herd of rutting moose! Who else could it be, eh? You timed things just right. My job's about done!" Hiram answered. "My body is telling me I should quit while I'm ahead. Here, help me stack these." While he straightened his shoulders and arched his back, I began to stack the wood he had just finished splitting.

"Stiff back?" I asked. Hiram was still stretching it out.

"If I take my time and relax these muscles once in a while, it's not too bad," he said.

"When you'd disappear from the village, you were coming here, weren't you?" I asked.

"I visit Awasosqua every so often," he explained.

"I'm still having dreams," I said. "The black wings are back." Hiram stopped stretching. "For how long?" he asked.

"They've been showing up the last few days now," I replied. "During the day I sometimes see the wings in the shadows. It's crazy, like Ki'kwa'jenu is waiting for me, playing with me like a cat plays with a mouse." I put another armful of firewood on the pile on the back porch and began to fit them into place. "I wish he'd go away."

"Spirit forms are not the same now," Hiram said.

"What do you mean?" I asked. I grabbed another armful of birch and began to make a crib to support the end of the pile.

"The wings you sometimes see belong to a Nighthawk that isn't as large as the spirit used to be ages ago," he explained. "Ki'kwa'jenu' once stood over ten feet tall," Hiram raised his hand straight above his head to approximate its height. "Moose were more than twenty feet tall. At least that's what the legends tell us."

"That's huge!" I said, finding it hard to believe my good friend. I was praying I wouldn't ever see a nighthawk or a moose that size.

"The Nighthawk of Molly's old village could be seen by everyone," Hiram explained. "Whenever it came, people hid in the brush. Sometimes, Ki'kwa'jenu flew off with someone, grasping the prize in its claws."

"That's awful! Where would it go?" I asked.

"Stories tell us that it has a nest near the top of one of the mountains just north of 'Suncook, hidden in the cliffs just above Longley beside Caucmagomic Mountain," Hiram answered. "Only a few have been able to escape. They returned with tales of human skulls littering the Nighthawk's nest, thighbones embedded in the sides like the sticks any other bird would build a nest with. None were ever the same."

"Didn't the spirit of Katahdin make creatures like the Nighthawk?" I asked.

"He did," Hiram replied," but he was really busy one day creating more rivers and lakes, and he turned over the task of creature management to Kabibonokka, spirit of the north wind. It was Kabibonokka who made all the creatures much larger than they are now. Beavers were taller than you are."

"That's pretty big," I said, "but what happened? No animal is so outsized now."

"Katahdin was so unhappy with Kabibonokka that he banished the spirit to the frozen land of the north. After sending him away, Katahdin reduced the size of all the creatures to what we see now. All except Ki'kwa'jenu. No one knows why, but because Katahdin was so busy fixing Kabibonokka's other mistakes, he overlooked the nighthawk. Over the centuries even the nighthawk began to shrink in size, but not by Katahdin's hand. No one knows why the nighthawk ended up the smaller size he is today." Hiram took out his briar pipe and began stuffing in some Prince Albert.

"Does the Nighthawk have any weakness?" I asked.

"Some think so, but nobody really knows. Ancient stories of those surviving his attacks tell how Ki'kwa'jenu could be kept at bay with a single eagle feather," Hiram explained, lighting his briar pipe and taking a few puffs to get it going. "Its power comes from his aerie. When the Nighthawk is far away from the nest, its power is weaker."

I tried to turn my mind away from screams, snapping bones, talons ripping my flesh on the flight to the nest. I was transfixed, staring blankly at the ax embedded in the chopping block only to be brought away from those images and sounds by Hiram.

"One old story tells how Ki'kwa'jenu could change into a different form," Hiram said.

That got my attention. "Like what forms?" I asked. That could be scary.

"Stories tell about it becoming a moose or deer. Some say a person," Hiram said.

"You think he wants me, don't you?" I asked.

"Seems like it," Hiram answered. "You seem to be the only one who sees the black wings today, but in the olden days, everyone could see the spirit and was terrified of it. Let me tell you what may happen and what you can do to protect yourself." Hiram talked more about Ki'kwa'jenu.

Molly and Abby walked out the back of the cabin to the woodpile where Hiram and I were standing, the screen door closing behind them with a bang that startled me. I had been lost in thought about the Nighthawk. "Walk with us," Molly said to me. "I need to see my patients." Hiram returned to chopping.

Abby and I followed her on a winding path covered by an arch of pine boughs. Like being in a cathedral, the sounds of our footsteps echoed above us. Sunlight and shadows danced around the treetops. A light wind from the south brought the promise of warmer weather and the smell of some needed rain. The trilling song of the winter wren reverberated through the forest, answered by the white-throated sparrow. There was such beauty in the forest if one knew where to look and how to listen.

We walked out of the woods to a barbed wire fence keeping some cattle safe from marauding bears. A narrow gate welcomed us to pass through. The cattle weren't even curious, and kept grazing on the newly sprouted grass. On the other side of the field was a small log cabin and an attached red barn, big enough for fifty horses at least. A compass rose was painted on the front above the double doors.

"Whose place is this?" Abby asked as we walked along a path that led toward the back of the barn.

"This is the Mitchell Farm," Grandmother Molly told us. "They buy and sell horses for woods and field work. Sometimes they'll train an ox or two. Their parents live with them. His father was chief of our clan for many years until he retired." We kept walking.

After we hiked past the barn and through the woods, we came to another clearing where there were several abandoned bunkhouses that had been logging camps. One of them was being used for the village's infirmary. It was set apart from the other buildings. Just in front of it was a red pitcher pump mounted on a rocked well, covered by a roof that supported a wooden crank, rope and bucket.

"These pails need filling." Molly said, "Bring them to the door and wait until I open it for you. I need to check the patients first, but do not come in by yourselves." I grabbed the pump handle while Abby set the first pail under the spout.

"It was nice of the Company," said Abby, "to leave these buildings for the villagers to use."

"I don't think it was on purpose," I said. "Father says the buildings are usually burned when they're done cutting. The woodsmen won't be back here for twenty or thirty years, and by then the camps wouldn't be worth much. I think they just forgot about them, there are so many areas where they're cutting."

"Good thing they did forget." We brought the pails of water to the building's entrance.

Molly appeared at the door. "Put those pails on that bench," she said through the screen as she pointed to a weathered gray bench, crudely made from three boards. "And wait here. I'll be right out. A few minutes passed. Wearing a bandana over her mouth and nose like one of the bandits that held up the shipment on Sias Hill, Molly handed us two bandanas.

"Put these on and try not to touch anything. This sickness is really contagious," Molly said. "We must be sure to wash our hands with lots of soap after we leave the building. Everyone is resting. Don't make any loud noises. Bright lights and noises are painful for these patients."

Abby and I brought the water pails inside and set them on a counter near a sink. I heard groans from the cots when I let the handle hit the side of the pail. There was a wood stove for heating in the center of the building, two pails of water resting on it steaming into the room. Each cot was curtained off from its neighbor. The only indication that patients were in the room were feet sticking out from under white sheets. I counted fifteen beds on each side, and all were occupied. I could hear coughing from the cots right in front of us. Several women were tending to the sick. It was clear that many were struggling to breathe. All the caretakers were wearing cloth masks over their faces and had on white cotton gloves.

"The greatest danger is from the fever, then there's difficulty breathing," Molly explained. "The medicine we need will knock the fever back and make it easier for them to breathe, but until we get it, we have to keep them cool with wet cloths and give them tea from willow bark." Willow bark tea contained the ingredient in aspirin. It was an ancient remedy. "Sometimes it helps them to breathe if we turn them over on their stomachs. There's nothing more we can do."

After Molly checked on her patients, we washed our hands at a station outside, ditched the bandanas in a basket outside the door and followed the path back. Hiram was still working on the firewood, the crack of his ax resonating between the little sheds nestled behind Molly's cabin.

"I need to show Abby how to use the amulet," Molly explained to me. "This would be a good time for you to take a walk around the village." I didn't mind being dismissed. I really wanted to check things out. This trip had become more dangerous than I could have imagined.

Skull Cave

chimney
light shaft over altar
skull face
exit
path to Old Village
enter
cavern
climb
path
light shaft
tunnel
cavern
to past & village
to present
altar
entrance
exit
tunnel
tunnel

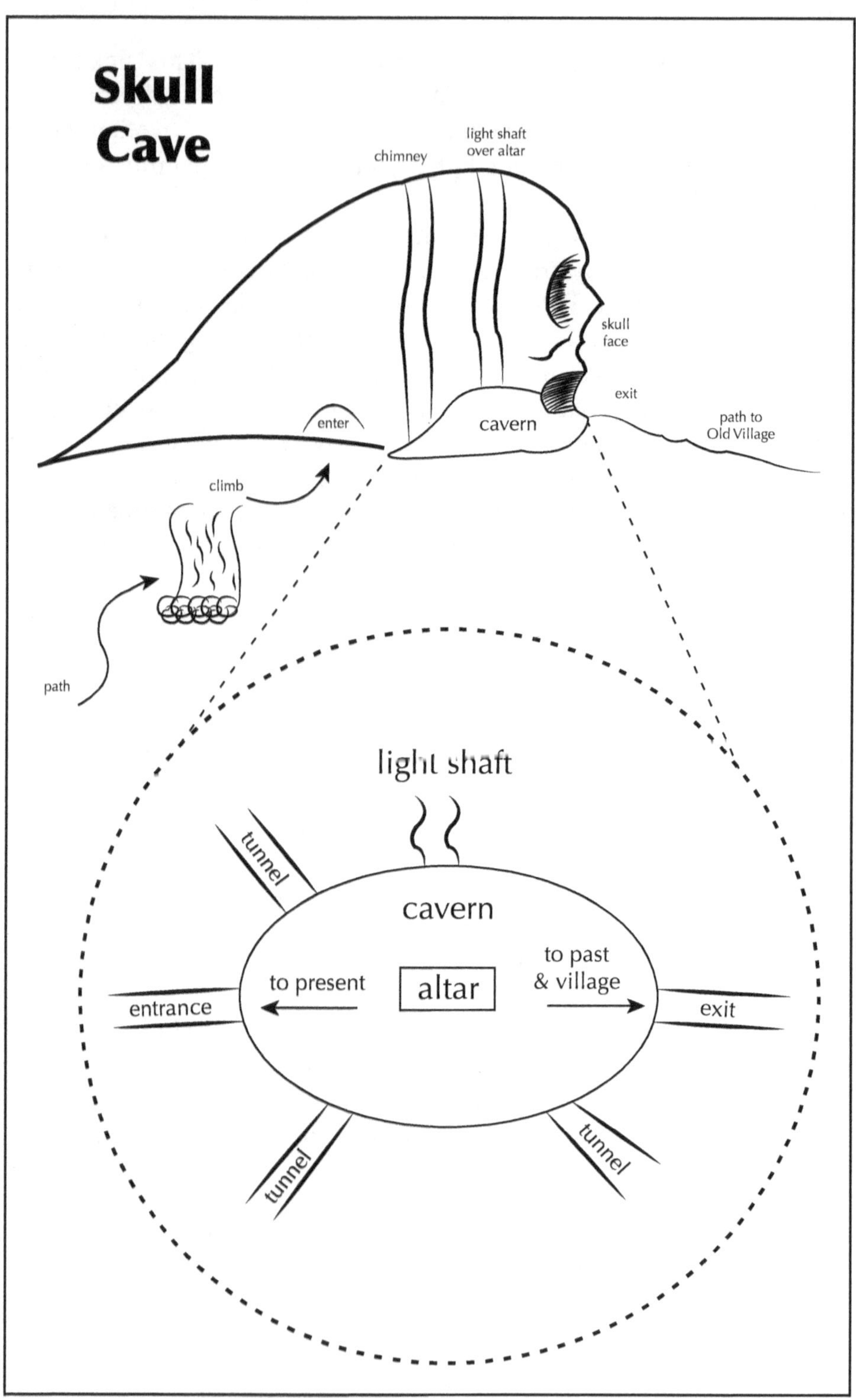

The Ceremony
Chapter 10

I walked back to the clearing and rested on an old stump. I could see the dwellings and people around the fire pit in the distance. I needed to think. Part of me didn't believe Grandmother Molly, but I did recognize I had something others did not. I was able to bring up a gale of a south wind. The first time it happened, a salmon I caught one winter slithered back into the ice hole, and that made me really mad. The sudden wind that came up blew me right to shore, sliding me over the clear ice. The second time was when the thugs from Boston threatened our family over our moonshine business. I was so angry that I caused a sudden windstorm that flipped their canoe. The men drowned, and we were safe for a while. The last time was when I learned Mother had died in the hotel fire. Most of the ashes blew away then, and the old white birch tree that had stood by the hotel for the last hundred years split apart and fell. Each time I was angry or afraid, I expressed myself without realizing what I was doing.

Since I did possess this crazy power that no one else seemed to have, why couldn't Grandmother Molly's story be true? While thinking about this, I felt a hand on my shoulder and jumped a bit.

"I didn't hear you coming," I said. I had wanted to be alone to think things through. Abby had startled me, and my tone was sharp.

"Charlie, I'm sorry I startled you," she said. "I know all of this is hard for you to accept, but let's not fight about it, okay? I can tell that this trip has been more of a challenge than you thought it would be. It has been for me, too, and it's far from over. The village needs us. Lives depend on us now."

I turned to look at her. Abby was the love of my life, I felt, but sometimes supporting her ideas was very difficult, especially now. Her dark eyes started to water. I stood up.

"I need your help, and the village needs your help," she said. "But I don't want all this to come between us."

I didn't say anything for a minute but nodded my head. We just looked at the village common, the smoke from the fire pit, the critter roasting on the spit, and the villagers waiting for dinner.

"I know," I finally said. "I want to do my part, but you know how I like things, nice and neat. This trip has been anything but!"

"Charlie, you wear your feelings on your forehead. It's easy to see. Let's head back to the cabin." I looked up at her as she reached down, offering her hand. I took it without hesitation and got up. We held each other for a moment. Then we walked quietly side by side, hand in hand back to the cabin. I love to be with Abby, and she has the kindest heart.

We found Molly sitting on the front steps with Hiram.

"Hiram and I think it's time that both of you take part in a ceremony before your journey."

"Journey? Ceremony?" I asked.

"Abby has agreed to help us," Hiram said. "She will travel a short distance to do so, and she needs you to go with her." I looked at Abby.

"It's important, isn't it?" I said. It was more of an observation than a question.

"Many lives are at risk," Hiram said.

"The ceremony is to recognize the special power you have, Charlie," Molly said. "Hiram told me about Sowanakik. Someday Abby will learn if she has a special ability. Our tribe will give you the task to find and return with the medicine. Everyone here is depending on you." Hiram was nodding his head in agreement.

"When is the ceremony?" Abby asked.

"Tonight, just after the feast. You will leave in the morning at sunrise," Hiram said.

Abby and I joined Molly and Hiram at the fire pit where the village shared the roasted beast with us. The illness didn't dampen their spirits. They seemed happy to be having some fun instead of staying in their homes, worrying about who was going to come down with the illness next. There were baked yams, potatoes, and a variety of breads. When we had our fill, the pipe was passed around the fire. Soon after, the drumming, singing and dancing began. Everyone wore the finest costumes. Silver medallions reflecting the firelight could be seen around the necks of many. There were beaver hats decorated with silver bands and others with tinsel and feathers of every description. Several wore wampum collars. The women had red, gold and green ribbons in their hair and on their dresses. I had never seen such a variety of color before. The scene looked like maple trees in their fall colors.

Hiram left to prepare for the ceremony. Abby and I were brought into a cabin where our faces were painted with red ochre and pale, gray clay. We wore hats that looked a lot like Molly's. Hiram's hat had different things hanging on it. I recognized several eagle feathers along with some blackbird and blue jay feathers, too. It looked like Hiram's ceremonial hat had been made from deer hide.

Abby and I followed Hiram into the center of the courtyard near the fire pit. There was a haze of sweet-smelling smoke in the air. Several men were drumming and singing. It was quite a sight with the firelight sending shadows across their painted faces while small sparks shot up into the clear, dark sky.

Hiram picked up a shallow wooden bowl that held sage and sweet grass braids. He lit both, and soon thick, white smoke began to rise. With a feather larger than any I had ever seen, he softly brushed the smoke away from the bowl numerous times, pushing the wisps here and there, changing his position on the compass so all the spirits would be pleased.

Then he walked over to us. I wasn't sure about the words he said, but while he was chanting, Hiram softly brushed a little smoke around each of us to clear away anything harmful from the spirit world. It was pretty overwhelming to stand there being brushed over with sweet smelling white smoke. I could feel the stress of our trip melt away, and I have felt the presence of serenity ever since.

After Hiram bathed Abby in the ceremonial smoke, he gave thanks for the animals, the fish, the forest, and asked the Great Spirit to protect us on our journey. We received ceremonial hats. Abby's was made from birch bark and looked a lot like Molly's with feathers and tufts of hair decorating it. Mine was made from an old bear skull, and wearing it gave me the sense of the beast that used to inhabit it. I became *Charlie Bear Claw*. Abby was given the name of *Morning Star*, both names chosen by Awasosqua.

The spirit Abby was named for was the daughter of Katahdin. She could make any wish come true. Red Rose, the wife of Katahdin, was also the mother of Lightning and Thunder, their only sons. I had to wonder if Uncle Amos named our oxen after them. Morning Star, their only daughter, married Waban, spirit of the East Wind in an elaborate ceremony with all the spirits attending.

When our ceremony finished, several of the villagers came up to congratulate us. Many wished us well with our journey. Hiram helped us put dishes of food away. There weren't many leftovers. Abby, Molly and I walked back to the cabin with Hiram. We cleaned off the face paint and sat down to talk about the next day.

"When should we leave?" asked Abby. If I'd learned anything about her, it had to be how fast she thinks about doing the next thing, and sometimes before the last thing is finished. I like to think first; Abby just dives right in.

"At first light. We have much to do tonight," Grandmother Molly said. "Hiram will help you collect what you need to make the trip. It's really important not to disturb the past except for gathering the plants we need."

Abby had been wearing the amulet since her grandmother had handed it to her earlier. She took it in her hand. The amulet seemed to glow at her touch, but no one mentioned it. Maybe it was only how the light reflected from it.

"I like how it feels in my hand." Abby turned the amulet over in her hand.

"It's the universe speaking to you," Grandmother Molly said. "The amulet has a way of letting you know if it likes your touch."

"How will we know what the plant looks like?" Abby asked.

"I have its cousin right here," Molly said, taking a book off the shelf above the table. She opened the book to the middle, and a flat group of leaves fell out.

"The plant you will be looking for is like this one but with yellow spots along the edges of the leaves. You should make a drawing to take with you." She handed the pressed leaves to Abby along with a blank piece of paper and pencil. She stood up, stretching her back as she did, and went to the stove.

Grandmother Molly fussed with the teakettle. There is a special place where the amulet may be used," she said to Abby. "There is an altar within the cavern, and on that altar is an indentation where the amulet must be placed."

"It can't be used anywhere else?" asked Abby.

"No," said Grandmother Molly. "The amulet will work only in its place in Skull Cavern. Charlie and Hiram will go pack while I teach you the secrets of the amulet. Then, you'll learn how to get into the cavern and what you may find on the other side."

"It's a half-day's travel to Split Rock. Once you locate the rock dome, you'll have to look around for the entrance tunnel," Hiram said as he stood up and motioned for me to come with him. We headed out the back door while Awasosqua reviewed the ritual Morning Star would need to perform while in the cavern.

"Split Rock is just that, a huge granite monolith that has been split in half by the winter's frost. See that ridge?" Hiram asked, pointing to the far horizon. It was easy to see, yellow moonlight glistening on the dark gray granite outcrops where Hiram pointed. "It doesn't look like much from here, but the view of the center outcrop looks like a skull sticking out from the trees." We began loading two pack baskets with provisions for the trip.

"That's why it's called the Skull Cave?" I asked anxiously.

Hiram turned toward me, a bag of pemmican in his hand, and smiled when he saw the concern on my face. "Some bear skulls have been found there over the years, but it gets its name from the outcrop resembling a human skull seen from the other side," Hiram explained. "It is said that long ago, the spirits of Katahdin created the cavern. It was their council chamber. They would meet there and decide the fates of the tribes and all the animals. The spirits would argue over what number of deer, moose and beaver would be enough to sustain them based on the offerings of each tribe."

"Fates of the animals were in the hands of the spirits?" I asked.

"That's the story that has come down to us," Hiram replied. "To be sure they were making the proper decisions, the spirits needed a way to look ahead so they could see what would happen if there were a drought, or big floods, or they made the beaver too large and so on. Katahdin ruled the spirit councils, and he created the altar and the ritual used to travel years forward or years in the past. When the amulet was given to Big Thunder's Beothuk tribe, it gave the holder the ability to travel in time."

Hiram turned to the packs on the porch. "It's a good idea to empty these pack baskets before you enter the cave," Hiram said." Then you'll have something to carry the plants in. I've put up some dried foods in case you have to stay overnight. These baskets are made in the old style and will not stand out. Your clothing needs to be different, though." He reached into his own pack basket and removed two sets of clothes and moccasins. "These should do it." Hiram handed me the clothes. "And I don't know how they'll react to Abby's red hair. She'll look different, and you're both tall, so that will make you both stand out."

"Maybe it won't be a problem," I said.

"Why not?"

"Remember the story you told me about the visits of the Vikings in the old times?" I asked.

"I remember telling you that. Do you think the red-haired visitors stayed for more than a quick raid and run?" Hiram cocked his head and looked at me closely.

"It wouldn't surprise me at all," I said. "Father told me about finding what he thought was the remains of a Viking shield at the north end of Caribou Lake."

"I saw that," Hiram said. "I don't know how anyone could tell what it was, but the rivets looked hand-made and what was left of the metal came from some really good steel maker to have lasted so long."

"So, maybe there'll be someone else then with red hair," I suggested.

"Well, I hope you're right." Hiram filled his pipe. "People who look different from everyone else are quickly singled out. You should dress before you enter the cave. Then, except for your height and maybe Abby's hair, you'll blend in pretty well when you arrive." He had thought of everything, and I grew a little less anxious.

"What could go wrong?" I asked. I was always thinking ahead for the unexpected. It was like scouting a rapid before trying to paddle it. It's a good idea to know what the options were in the journey ahead, but in this case, anything could go wrong.

"It's risky, but when Abby performs the ritual correctly, you'll be fine. The risk is greatest when you're in the old village," Hiram continued. "You have to hide or fit in. The language may be a little different, and that means you'll need to limit your contact with people while you look for the plants."

"Olive has been teaching us the old language," I said. "We've learned a lot of their words and phrases." Going back to the old village was beginning to sound pretty interesting. I was wondering what would be different.

"Olive is an expert in the old tongue," Hiram said. "And you couldn't ask for a better teacher." I hoped he was right. It would be bad if we got there, didn't fit in, and couldn't understand much. We'd attract too much attention and language tends to change over time.

"There's another concern we have in sending you there," Hiram said. "You may carry disease that could devastate the old village. It's important that you not get too close to anyone there."

"We'll be sure to keep our distance," I said.

"You'll have a drawing of the plant, so you'll recognize it. We also have a similar plant to go by. Molly said.

It wasn't long before Abby and Molly joined me and Hiram on the back porch. Abby had a packet wrapped in oil cloth under her arm. Grandmother Molly handed Abby a handful of green moss wrapped in birch bark. "This is the cousin to the plant you need to find. The leaves are the same in shape, but the one you are looking for is yellow in color with large white and black spots, not orange ones. The one that grows here now doesn't have the same healing magic. Be sure to take all of the root and fill each basket at least halfway."

"Why aren't the plants you need growing here now?" Abby asked.

"I'm afraid Charlie Bear Claw is right," Grandmother Molly said. She looked at me with a smile and a slight nod that told me she felt the same way. "There are other reasons why some species of animals or plants thrive or die off over the centuries, but this extinction doesn't seem to be naturally caused." I wondered what else would be different then, and I was looking forward to finding out.

We finished loading our packs. Hiram looked over the clothing again, and we took the packs to the little bunkhouse out back where Abby and I would stay the night. At first light we would get the rest of the directions to the Skull Cave and say our good-byes.

Hiram called to us. Molly wanted us in the kitchen to share some tea before we turned in.

"I've hesitated to ask," Abby began. "I know we will be meeting Nolka, but will Charlie and I meet your father?"

"I hope you will," she sighed. "You'll arrive just a day or two after I left, so he should be there." She smiled at the thought of her father. "If you happen to meet him, his name is 'Wobe Moulsem'."

"'Gray Wolf'?" Abby asked.

"Yes, 'Gray Wolf'," Molly explained.

"How will we know who he is?" asked Abby.

"He wore his long, gray hair tied behind his head," came the reply. "You'll recognize a carved ivory clasp holding it in place. It's identical to mine." Molly whipped around her hair to show us the clasp she wore. "No one else has one. The clasps came from a clan living near the ocean. I think they came from a walrus or a whale." The clasp was intricately carved.

"If we do meet him, is there a message you'd like us to give him?" I asked.

She thought a moment. "Tell him I am well and have had a good life. Thank him for sending me here. I've missed him."

"We're supposed to arrive shortly after he sent you away," I said. "Is it possible that we could arrive before that happened and meet your younger self if we arrived any sooner?"

"With the right words, yes," she said. "But part of the ritual I have taught Abby prevents that from happening.

"What if we don't get back to the right time?" I asked.

"That doesn't happen often," Molly explained, "but if it does, you have to go back to the cavern and repeat the ritual. Maybe the spirits weren't listening too carefully the first time." That made me more anxious; now I worried about not getting home again.

We spent the rest of the evening learning about some other customs of her clan, and Molly taught us some new words and phrases we might need. Grandmother Molly warned us about the crystal.

"Although I don't think it would happen, you will want to be certain not to allow the crystal to come into contact with the amulet," she said in a stern voice. "That can cause trouble in the spirit world."

"What trouble?" Abby asked.

"The spirits never liked us to have more power than they did, and both talismans held by the same person does just that. Katahdin's spirits may come for you," Molly explained. "And it may become difficult to defend yourselves against them."

"We'll be careful," we said at the same time.

On our way back to the bunkhouse, I looked up at the stars. There was Ursa Major, the constellation of the bear, clearly in the North sky. I remembered hearing that the stars' positions change over time, that the ancient peoples who first settled the land here saw a different arrangement of stars than the one I was looking at. Soon enough, I might get to see the difference myself.

There were no black wings of Ki'kwa'jenu in my dreams that night.

Skull Cave
Chapter 11

We had an early breakfast with Grandmother Molly and Hiram. After, we got the rest of the directions for our journey.

"Once you pass Split Rock, the trail becomes harder to follow," Grandmother Molly explained. "There is a waterfall that can be seen just before the cave's entrance. We call it Horse Tail Falls. The path to the cave is hidden behind the falls."

We strapped on our pack baskets. There was some fussing with the right adjustments, and in a minute we were off.

"Travel safely," Hiram said.

"May the spirits be with you," Grandmother Molly said.

"We'll see you soon," we said.

We set off to find the cave, turning around briefly for a parting wave to her, Hiram and some other members of the tribe who had come to see us off. The sickness had spread, making the success of our journey more critical as the hours passed. One more member of their village had died during the night. We didn't have much time.

The anxious feeling that welled up whenever I was about to do something risky nearly overcame me while we followed the path to the river's edge. Would we be able to return? Only Abby knew how to get back, and she held the amulet. Abby knew the words to say, but I wasn't told the complex ritual. What if something happened to her? The amulet? What would that be like, I wondered, stuck in a time when there were daily challenges for survival, but of a different nature? We wouldn't know the language or most of their customs, and I had no skills of value. We'd be just a burden on their food supplies. I didn't know how to make an arrowhead. When exploring the lakeshores I picked up many arrowheads, both finished and broken. Most showed amazing craftsmanship in the thinness of the finished product, arrowheads nearly translucent. There were no doctors beyond their medicine man, just herd immunity to whatever sickness came along. There were no bucksaws to cut a winter's supply of wood, no steel axes to split it with and no kerosene or wooden matches to get it going. I was going to see first-hand how the tribes followed and hunted the animals that followed the browse as post-glacial forests grew, how they were able to survive in the land of snow. There would be lots to learn. Everything would be different.

We paddled the canoe across the stream and stashed it on the other side under some brush. The paddles went underneath, and we hoisted our pack baskets, walking down a clearly defined trail. After we passed through a stand of old growth pines, we came to a little rise. In the distance we could see several mountains and smaller peaks.

Molly and Hiram had described the route well, even though they had not traveled in that direction for a long time. It was Abby who first saw the rock that marked the way.

"That has to be Split Rock," she said. "It's about the right height and that cedar is really big."

"And old," I added. Before us was a large gray boulder, twice my six-foot height. It had been split almost in two equal halves. Moss and lichen grew down from the top. An old cedar tree, its bark deeply furrowed, grew between them, but it was its ancestors and winter's ice that had done the splitting. Over the centuries, successive trees pushed the halves apart a little more each year.

I looked up. "See that?" I said, pointing to the top of the cedar.

"See what?" Abby said.

"A raven's nest," I said and pointed. "There, at the top. It's pretty big. See it?"

Abby looked up. "I thought it was part of the tree. I can barely make it out," Abby said. "Wait, I think there's a raven in it now." The black bird's sudden cawing warned others there were strangers about as it flew from the treetop.

"What's that shiny thing on the side of the nest?" Abby asked, pointing up the tree.

"Ravens collect shiny objects. I don't know why they do it, but it's pretty common. Maybe that's what it is, a piece of bottle glass or something. They decorate their nests like we decorate our homes," I explained.

"Better keep this amulet out of sight," Abby laughed. "Don't want any ravens attacking me," she joked.

"Hey, we'd better be going if we're going to get back before dark," I said.

We managed to squeeze past the old cedar trunk. It wouldn't do to get a foot stuck here, and I could see that happening if one wasn't paying close attention or slipped at the wrong moment. You could get trapped here and no one would ever know it until your bones were found, if they were found. The trail turned into a narrow animal path.

When we got past the rock, we looked for the waterfall Molly told us was just beyond, and we saw its silver streak pouring over a cliff in the distance. The ridgeline that Hiram had pointed out in the moonlight last night was right beside it. A nearly bare dome of solid rock rose at some distance just above the trees. As we got closer, I thought I could see the profile of a skull near a cliff. By the looks of the terrain, it would take over an hour's hike to get there. Boulders strewn everywhere in an ancient glacial riverbed that would lead us to our destination meant that there would be lots of jumping from one big gray rock to another with water trickling in between. Our heavy packs made the trek a bit harder. I didn't see how we were going to accomplish our goal and return by dark. This hike was taking longer than we thought. After another hour, we got a good look at the ridge.

"I think the cave entrance is ahead," Abby said, pointing to an outcrop of rock at the base of the hill we were heading to. We could see the waterfall, and now we had to find the path behind it.

"I hope so, 'cause my feet are getting sore," I complained.

"You're such a big baby," she teased. Her freckles seemed to laugh at me. I had to smile a little. I knew she didn't really mean it.

Big, fluffy gobs of clouds scooted by, blown south by a strong Canadian front that blasted through, bringing colder air, and putting an end to the occasional rain and thunder showers of the last two days.

Looking down the valley, we could see the smokestacks of the mills, rows of tiny streets and miniature homes. Soon, we reached the falls and crawled over some pretty slippery rocks as we made our way behind the curtain of water. There were veins of white and yellow quartz running through the rock walls surrounding us. We searched for the cave opening that Molly described. Abby dove into a thicket of mountain ash and young fir that was trying to carve out an existence while stuffed into a crack in the solid rock.

"Here it is!" she shouted from the brush. Behind the brush was the mouth of a tunnel, barely large enough for us to slither through. "What should we do with all our gear?" she asked me.

"Hiram said we should take only the dried food. We'll need to stash the rest here. I hate to leave the rifle," I complained.
"It's just not a good idea to bring it with us," Abby said. "We can't take the chance to have it fall into the wrong hands in the wrong time."

"Yeah, you're right," I conceded. "We'll have to make a torch so we can see in the cave, and we'll need the nearly empty packs for the plants."

"There's a good place over there," she pointed out. We stashed our gear and most of our provisions behind a boulder near the entrance, and Abby made another birchbark torch.

"Anything else you can think of that we'll need?" I asked.

"Let's take some matches. We have the stone knives Hiram made for us." Hiram was an expert flint knapper who could make a stone tool in less than five minutes. Abby pushed the bushes aside. "Hey, what's this?" she asked, holding up a handful of black, coarse hair.

"Looks like some critter came by not long ago," I said. I didn't like enclosed spaces much, but I couldn't seem to come up with a good excuse to back out of the plan now when lives were at stake.

Abby lit one of the three torches we made, and we peered down into the tunnel. We couldn't see a thing beyond the immediate opening, it was so black inside.

Abby took off her pack basket and went first, crawling on the floor of pine needles. "Hey, I can stand up," she shouted back to me. "Slide the packs to me," she asked. "I thought we were going to have to crawl all the way through."

"These cave walls are pretty smooth," I pointed out. "Except for a little pocket here and there, it's pretty straight. And I'm not seeing many cobwebs."

"Don't think anyone broom swept it, do you?" She joked.

"Very funny. Maybe spiders aren't allowed," I kidded back. "I sure hope there aren't any bats living here." I wasn't a fan of either bats or spiders.

As the torch pushed back the darkness, we moved farther into the cave. The feeble light from the lantern showed a rock or two strewn in our path. We hadn't been walking very long, feeling our way along the smooth sides of the tunnel and looking for loose rocks that might come down on us. The tunnel was musty smelling, rock walls glistening with moisture as the torch lit our way. Unexpectedly, the darkness began to fade.

"Look, there's some light ahead," Abby said, pointing to a small circle on the floor that was illuminated, and not by our torch. We looked up. Almost right above us was a crevasse that seemed to lead to the outside. Crisscrossing the chimney-like crevasse, cedar roots looked like rungs on a ladder.

"Do you hear something?" Just as I asked, I got a strong whiff of bear. "And that smell?"

"Oh-oh," Abby said, wrinkling her nose at the scent.

Then the bear spoke. Its roar was the loudest, angriest thing I had ever heard. Every hair on my neck, my back, and my head stood up on end. A trembling of fear swept over me.

"We'd better back out now," I said. "I see two small cubs hiding in the shadows." We stepped back, making some distance from the roaring beast as fast as we could. Soon, we were back at the cave's opening.

"What now?" Abby said. "We have to get through that cave, but I don't think the bear is going to let us."

"Remember that crevasse we saw? Maybe we can find the opening up top and drop this torch down the chimney. The fire will frighten the bear, and it will leave. I'll hide near the entrance to watch it go. I'll yell when it's clear for us to go back in and find the cavern and stone altar." It all seemed so simple to me.

"Wouldn't she come back?" Abby asked.

"Fire is pretty scary for animals," I explained. "That bear won't be coming back."

Abby hiked to the top of the dome where she found the opening we had seen from the inside. She dropped her now blazing torch down the hole.

I hid beside the entrance, and in just a minute the bear came racing out, fur smoking and two little cubs trailing right on its heels. I shouted, "All clear!" and Abby joined me at the entrance. We found our way back inside.

We passed by the dropped torch. It was still smoking on the cave floor. There was a strong smell of burned hair. I picked it up and re-lit it from the one she was carrying.

"How far does this go?" I asked.

"Until it meets the other tunnels," she said. Grandmother was specific about how several tunnels met in one wider place in a larger cavern.

"Are we sure this isn't a dead end?" I asked.

"Why?"

"Because I think we have company, and that bear doesn't seem happy." I turned with the torch. The bear had come back to settle up with its tormentor by tearing limbs and such. The roar became louder. My hair stood higher. The bear was getting closer. Again.

"Quick," I said, as I leaned my torch against the cave wall. "On my shoulders and up the chimney." Abby threw her torch on the ground and didn't waste any time climbing up my back.

"Hurry, darn beast is getting closer," I said. We were lucky that we didn't have to dump our pack baskets; the escape route above us was wide enough so we could keep them on our backs. I gave Abby's foot one final boost above my head.

Abby pulled herself up hand over hand, grabbing more roots as she ascended the crevasse, root by root, climbing towards the light. I reached for the first root above the cave's ceiling. The passage was just wide enough so we could keep our packs on.

"She has cubs, and that's not good. Hurry it up!" she screamed over her shoulder, now half-way to the top. "And I really hate these cobwebs." The crevasse seemed to have been reserved just for spiders. Good thing she went first, clearing the cobwebs away as she went. I hated them more.

The bear came closer. I started to pull myself up the chimney when I caught some movement in a little side pocket. There, waking up, was one more bear cub who had been left behind. Mama had come back for it.

"Okay, so there's another cub. Here I come." I pulled myself up. The bear roared again, teeth moving toward me faster than I would like, me, a tasty treat between her and her baby.

The moment I grabbed a cedar root and gave myself a good lift, mama bear swatted my foot. One of her toenails scraped my heavy boot and jerked me back down a few inches. Just as the bear was about to make another swipe at my boot, I made one more pull, now safe from claws and teeth.

We got to the top of the chimney, dragging ourselves out onto a flat rock. Abby reached down and gave me a hand. For a moment, we were breathless.

"They're afraid of fire? Right!" she said. I didn't appreciate her sarcasm. It was a few moments before we calmed down and we could talk without being out of breath.

"What about a different entrance? Didn't Grandmother Molly say something about another tunnel?" I asked. We had brushed off the dirt and cobwebs from the chimney. The claw rake on my boot showed how close I had come to being dinner.

"She did say there was an exit tunnel to travel to the old times, but we're not supposed to go in that way. Maybe we should take a look around." Abby scurried off like a mountain goat to another side of the dome before I could say anything. Dutifully, I looked about in the other direction.

"I found a notch we can climb up!" she shouted from the edge of a cliff. Hanging on to more roots didn't thrill me too much, but we pulled ourselves up, using rocks along the sides and the occasional root, being careful with our footing.

"Hey!" I yelled, brushing off dirt from my head. Abby was above me, and her last foot hold sent gravel cascading down on me.

"Sorry," she said. "Wait until I get all the way up there before you move again."

When Abby reached the top of the notch, I clawed myself up to where she was standing.

I followed her along a cut across the ledge and up the otherwise smooth ledge until we ran into some bushes. Beyond them was an opening large enough to squeeze through sideways.

"I think we should try this," she said.

"Okay," I agreed, but I wasn't feeling too great about climbing inside a cave where mama bear could be waiting for us.

We squeezed through the opening. In front of us was darkness blacker than was natural. The gloom had sucked up all the light around and hungered for more. Abby lit another torch. A long, straight tunnel opened in front of us at a downward slope, the sides wet and smoothly polished. There were a few rocks on the floor in front of us, and the passage was high enough to stand up straight at first. This tunnel didn't smell like bear like the last one did, and I was a little relieved. The bear probably hadn't come this way.

"Let's see where this one goes," she said, brushing away more cobwebs. "We'll have to climb down." It wasn't far before the shaft ended. From the torchlight, we were able to see a large opening just below. It was a drop of eight feet to the floor, but using the last few outcrops of rock, we lowered ourselves into the cavern safely. I could see two tunnels right away, one smaller than the other but as we looked around, we could see others. Grandmother Molly was right. This cavern was a meeting place of several access tunnels. They came together like the spokes of a wheel.

"At least there's no bear," I said.

"Well, not yet anyway," she agreed. I just stared at her. I couldn't wait to get outside. "Look, that's it!" Abby pointed to a coffin shaped block of stone, raised on a pile of flat rocks. We walked over to it, its surface glowing yellow from the torch light. Someone had gone to a lot of work carving out two footprints in the large, flat stones that outlined the base of the altar.

"Here, hold this up so we can see the top of the stone." After she handed over her torch, she reached around her neck and brought out the amulet Grandmother had given her. Petroglyphs were carved along the altar's top and face.

"Should we really be doing this?" I asked. "I mean, what if something happens and we don't get back?"

We had talked some about the journey we were about to take, what would happen to the present if something changed in the past, a conversation we had had several times already. We would have to be careful.

"Nothing bad will happen," she said. "We'll focus on what we need to do." Abby's tone was more hopeful than reassuring. "Remember, there are many who are depending on us."

"Which tunnel is the one we were supposed to come in through?" I asked. I couldn't tell which was which, but there were two larger ones at opposite ends.

"Grandmother Molly said the entrance and exit tunnels we're supposed to use are at opposite ends," Abby said.

"But which two?" I asked.

"She said it was the larger ones. The large one to the left of the altar is the entrance from our side where the bear lives, and the one to the right is the exit to the old times."

Surrounded by more glyphs in the center of the stone block was a round indentation, just the right size for the amulet. Grandmother Molly told Abby what words to say after placing the amulet there and the correct orientation for it rest on the altar. Anyone Abby was touching during the ceremony came with her, so she grabbed my hand as she spoke the phrases she had learned. Then, we stood quietly. I could still hear water dripping somewhere. Nothing happened.

"That's strange," she said. "I thought at least there would be something, a flash of light maybe."

"Or another bear?" I offered. "Maybe it's time we went back." She looked at me, sighed and shook her head.

"Maybe you're right. I guess I could have messed up the ritual," she said, reaching for the torch in my hand. "Does it seem colder in here? I can see my breath. I wish I had my winter coat. Let's go check." Abby put the amulet back safely around her neck and led us through the opposite tunnel toward the faint light at the other end.

Below us was an ice-cold world of white. Arctic-like gusts occasionally whipped snow past the cave's opening. When the view cleared a little between gusts, I couldn't see any trees, just miles and miles of white. I couldn't see any mountains where there should be plenty of tall peaks. There was no paper mill, no smokestacks, no tiny streets, no miniature homes, no nothing except for a whiteness that stretched as far as I could see.

"Hey, maybe we'll see a polar bear," I quipped. "Did you remember the snowshoes?" I could be pretty sassy when stressed out, and I was feeling a bit of stress now. "And it's really cold, too."

Abby replied by shaking her head. "Let's go back and try it again. I'm getting really cold really fast." I couldn't feel my toes, and my fingers weren't far behind. We ran back to the cavern. I guess things could be worse and we could have run into dinosaur! I was hoping we didn't have to slog through five-foot drifts without snowshoes. "Okay," I shivered. "Why aren't the seasons the same?"

"Maybe it's the same month, but we went so far back there are still glaciers around Mt. Katahdin," Abby suggested. Things did look pretty well frozen up for May.

Abby and I stood at the stone altar once more, her ice-cold fingers fumbling with the amulet. Abby went through the ritual once more while I held the torch and her hand. Again, there was nothing to indicate anything had happened until we felt hot, fetid air when we approached the end of the tunnel. Before us was a very different world. The air was hazy. The riverbeds were bone dry. I could see no mill, no houses but I could make out a chimney here and there where houses had once been. It looked like we could be far in the future. There were no trees, but very short ferns that grew in a carpet as far as we could see in the thick air that smelled like rotten eggs. I thought I spied a palm tree at the edge of the foggy mist. We began coughing. The air was so foul, hot and damp all at the same time. No living thing could survive in this time.

"I can't breathe!" I said, choking. "Let's get out of here!"

"Okay, once more," Abby said, coughing hard. "But we should hurry. I don't know how long we should be breathing this bad air." I was already getting dizzy. We raced back to the cavern once more. The air around the altar seemed better, and it soothed our lungs that had been irritated by the toxic atmosphere outside. Abby stood before the altar again. She leaned against the stone, her coughing subsided, and she went through the ritual again, slower this time, holding on to me. Again, nothing occurred to indicate we had been successful in reaching the targeted time, but the air suddenly seemed easier to breathe as we approached the exit.

"I hope that's not our future," Abby said as we saw daylight filtering in from the tunnel's opening.

"It might be if we keep putting poisons in our air and water," I said. "It looked like there was no life at all, no town, no mill, nothing."

"Maybe we could do something to prevent it?" Abby asked.

"What, keep people from getting rich? Yeah, that should be an easy thing to do!" I said. We had reached the opening at the tunnel's entrance. The sun seemed brighter and the air smelled like fish.

Neither of us was prepared for what we saw when we reached the opening in the side of the cliff.

Ndakina
(Homeland)
Chapter 12

When I first saw the forest spread out over a plateau below us, I wondered if we had traveled to a different planet. I'd seen tall trees before when cruising for timber with Uncle Amos and Father. Those were called "old growth pine," but these pines were much higher and thicker at the trunk. Four people standing around one wouldn't be able to touch their outstretched hands. There were no branches littering the forest floor. There was so much room between them that it would be easy enough to ride a horse at a gallop.

"Those trees are as tall as the giant redwoods we saw pictures of in school!" Abby exclaimed.

"I remember seeing them," I said. It was easy to make out some details of the village since the maples surrounding the buildings were only beginning to leaf out. At least we had arrived in the same season, I thought.

"Look at those long houses," I said. "Everything seems so neat." In a mesa-like clearing below us stood dome shaped huts and long houses with arched roofs, sheathed with bark from white birch and cedar. Laced between upright poles, the bark shingles easily shed the water and snow. Light wisps of smoke came from the tops of some. A small stream flowed near the entrance and along the side farthest from us. We could see several longer structures, some with more than one opening in the roof to carry away smoke from the cooking fires within. Garden plots were here and there, but all their rows went in the same direction. It was as if someone had taken an iron rake and used it to draw patterns in the sand.

"This is amazing," Abby said. "Do you see that fence?" A meandering stockade fence enclosed the entire village, no doubt to keep the wandering bears, raccoons and groundhogs from devouring their crops and raiding their stores of food. Criss-crossed saplings thatched over with bark, like their homes made the stockade look like it had been constructed with very wide boards nailed between thick posts.

"Where are we?" Abby asked. "Is this the Ndakina Grandmother Molly told us about?"

"I'm wondering when we are," I replied. "It might be her homeland." I could see many people burying what looked like fish around tall stakes in the gardens. Along the edges of the fencing were drying racks of pink salmon fillets larger than anything we had ever caught.

"I was hoping the air would be sweeter," I said. The aroma from the drying fish was wafting up the hill. There was a game pole near an opening in the fence. A moose, two deer, one of which was an albino, and a few brown rabbits were hanging from it.

I had kept Father's pocket spyglass even though Grandmother Molly thought we should bring nothing with us from our time. We had already brought matches to make it easy lighting torches. If something foreign to the era were found, there might be a problem, but I had a feeling that we would need the glass, and it was worth the risk.

All the homes were arranged in concentric half-circles around a large fire pit and totem pole. Using the glass, I could see details of their houses and some faces of those in the courtyard. A man with three black feathers in the back of his headband came toward the door of one of the longer houses facing the central courtyard.

"I think I see Blackfeather," I said, handing the glass to Abby. "Look to the center of the back row. It's a long house."

"That could be him," Abby agreed. "There are two men beside the door. They're removing a pole that was jamming the door closed. Now he's going inside. Here, check out the ornaments around the door." She handed the glass back.

"Yup, those are some pretty big black feathers," I said. "Wait, he's coming out." Blackfeather came back through the doorway, and the two men put the pole back in place. "This guy has guards and keeps his place locked. Wonder what's inside?"

"More like who's inside?" Abby asked.

"I don't know," I said. "Maybe. Here, take another look."

"I think he's wearing a necklace…looks like claws!" Abby handed the glass back.

"Okay, I see him." I said. "Hey! Those aren't claws, they're hawk's talons! And big ones, too! Blackfeather has some company. Two men just joined him. It looks like they're getting some spears together. I think they're going out hunting. Do you want to head down?" I asked.

"We should wait and watch for Nolka. Then we ask her to help us find the plants like the samples we brought with us."

"Those lessons we've had from Olive?" I asked. "How could the language be the same so long ago? At all?"

"Olive has taught us a lot, Charlie. Remember what she said?" Abby asked. "The ancient language was preserved because it was tied to the land, the culture and is still spoken in ceremonies today." Abby reached into her pack and pulled out an oilcloth covered packet. "These drawings Grandmother Molly and I made will help, too."

"You have skills," I said. "Next, you'll tell me you can travel through time," I joked.

"Funny guy," she said. "Let's not lose sight of why we're here."

"Yeah, I hope we can get back in time, and in the right time," I said. "I don't think I want to live here."

We took turns watching. After an hour had passed, I saw a girl a few years younger than Abby walk across the clearing with two children in tow. The kind of containers she and the children were carrying gave away their errand. They were going for water from a little stream just outside the gate. Her clothing seemed ornamental with beaded designs over the shoulders and intricate fringes from her arms and waist. Others who passed by greeted her in a friendly way. We were pretty sure this was Nolka.

"There's something around her neck that's reflecting the sun," Abby observed. "I think that could be the crystal!"

"Then she has to be Running Deer," I said.

We hoisted our packs and crept down the incline toward a side opening in the stockade fence that surrounded the village. It was tough to do this with the brush in our way. Some large boulders here and there were large enough for us to hide behind. Then, there were some large trees. No one else was on the path to the small stream. We watched for her. It wasn't long before she passed by, the two children laughing and following close behind.

Abby and I met them at the stream. Nolka froze when she saw us standing in front of her.

"Greetings, Nolka," Abby said.

"Awasosqua!" Nolka cried out, a look of surprise on her face. Abby must have looked a lot like her much younger grandmother.

"No, Nolka, my name is Abby Morning Star," she said in the old language Grandmother Molly had taught us. "Awasosqua is my grandmother." Nolka stared at Abby, confusion on her face.

"Awasosqua gave me this," Abby said, showing Nolka her amulet, "so we could come here."

"I know she had to travel with the amulet," Nolka said, "but she hasn't been gone long enough to have a granddaughter. She left just three nights ago!"

"Time's passing isn't the same for everyone," I said. "She's much older now." Nolka was having a difficult time understanding how her sister, not much older than she was a few days earlier, was now a grandmother. There must have been some fast current in the time stream Grandmother Molly jumped into!

"The amulet is very powerful," Nolka said with a sigh. "Strange things can take place when using it, so I guess it could happen." She stared at the amulet and put her hand over the crystal hanging from her neck. "This crystal is also very powerful. It protects me from evil some spirits can do."

"Awasosqua told us about it. She also said we must never let them touch. Has Blackfeather bothered you at all?" Abby asked.

"No, he has stayed away from me," she said.

"This is Charlie Bear Claw," I said. Nolka nodded her head in my direction and smiled.

"He is really tall," she smiled. Abby nodded her head. I was used to comments about my height and said nothing.

"Is my sister well?" Nolka asked. "We miss her terribly. Nolka dropped her head, sniffled and wiped a tear from her cheek with a sigh. She looked at Abby again, and without waiting for a reply, she said, "Your hair is as red as Sly Fox's!"

"I get it from Awasosqua's side of the family," Abby explained. "She is well and has a good life," Abby replied. "She misses you very much, Nolka." Abby reached into her pack basket and removed the folded oil cloth.

"She asked for your help in finding these," Abby explained, unfolding the water-tight packet holding similar leaves and then showing Nolka a drawing of the plant we sought. "Can you tell us where we can find these? Awasosqua said they could be in Kabibonokka's Canyon, but we don't know where that is."

"She's alright? It's not for her?" Nolka asked again, looking up from the sketch in her hands. She must have known about the plant's medicinal properties just from Grandmother Molly's request, and from her frown, I guessed that Nolka knew about the sickness it could cure.

"She's fine, but many members of her tribe are sick. Some have died. She sent us here to harvest the plant and bring it back to her so she can make the medicine that will cure them," Abby explained. "It no longer grows anywhere in our time." Nolka nodded her head. Abby folded up the drawing and re-sealed the oil cloth packet.

"These can be found only at the very end of Kabibonokka's Canyon," Nolka confirmed, handing the drawings back to Abby.

"Follow this stream," she said. "Its source is where the plants grow between the willow trees. It is a difficult journey since the recent anger of Blackfeather brought down many giants. Be careful with fire. There is no way out except the way you go in."

"Blackfeather's anger brought down trees?" I asked. I knew a little about anger and the wind, but who was this guy?

"Moosis can tell you," Nolka said. "Moosis, Little Bezo!" The two youngsters appeared in an instant. "This is Abby Morning Star and her friend, Charlie Bear Claw. She is your cousin from far away, Moosis. And this is Little Bezo. His grandfather is Old Bezo, who leads the clan at Schunk'awke." The children smiled and said hello. "Moosis, tell your cousin about what you saw the other day."

"I saw Blackfeather walk by some women. I heard giggling and saw them pointing at his long nose, beady eyes and long, thin face. They were laughing at his rejections and were making fun of how he was able to convince Mahtagwaysoo's father to give her to him in marriage." Moosis took a breath. "After they passed by, he walked to the mouth of Kabibonokka's canyon. I followed him as I hid behind trees along the pathway there. When he came to a clearing, he stopped and roared like an angry beast. It was so loud. I was afraid."

"I would have been, too," I said. "What happened then?"

"Kabibonokka came roaring down the mountain's face, down over the high cliffs that make the canyon, and flattened a lot of sacred trees." Moosis looked at Nolka.

"Have you told Gray Wolf yet?" Running Deer asked.

"I told him right away," he said, "on my way back." Moosis and Bezo ran up the stream beside us.

"Who's being kept in Blackfeather's long house?" Abby asked.

"Mahtagwaysoo. Someone who brought in food for her yesterday and told me that Blackfeather kept her locked in the back room," Nolka said. "Her father gave her away for a promise of good hunting; there's nothing to be done. Blackfeather kept his promise and the hunting has been wonderful lately. The marriage ceremony is tonight"

"We should do something to help her," Abby said to me.

"That isn't the job we're supposed to be doing!" I said in English so Nolka wouldn't understand. I worried that Abby wanted to save the world again, like she did by running up onto that log jam at Rymes' Pitch.

"Okay, Charlie, I know. I guess we should go." Abby looked at Nolka.

"Thank you for telling us the way, Nolka. It would be best that no one else knew we were here, especially Blackfeather," Abby said. When she heard Blackfeather's name, Nolka's face darkened.

"He's a bad man," Nolka said. "I agree. It would be best to stay far away from him."

"We should go," I said. Abby and I turned to leave.

"Bezo!" she shouted. "Moosis!" They ran back to her side, giggling on the way.

"Give my love to Awasosqua," Nolka embraced Abby, then me. We began to follow the stream to Kabibonokka's Canyon, turning to wave good-bye to Nolka, Moosis and Little Bezo as they continued to fetch water from the stream.

"Did you get a good look at the crystal pendant around her neck?" I asked when we walked away.

"I did. The crystal seemed to glow when she touched it," Abby observed. "She's lucky she has it. She and the children seem fine."

"Grandmother Molly will be pleased to hear," I said. "We need to get going." We adjusted our packs and started down the trail Nolka had pointed to.

We followed a well-used path along the stream, stopping for something to eat under a canopy of budding maple leaves. The moss was so thick that it was like sitting on a soft, thick green cushion. I took off my moccasins and soaked my feet in the cold water of a large pool that the river had carved out between the canyon walls. We looked at the canyon's shape. Tall, sheer cliffs were on each side of us now. It would be impossible to climb out. Following the path along the stream was the only way in or out.

"Looks like the results of Blackfeather's anger," I said. I was looking at a cedar that had been uprooted. Usually, larger cedars had strong root systems, so the wind that brought this one down was pretty strong. We continued along the stream.

"Do you think we'll be back on the other side of the cavern by dark?" I asked. Abby stopped short.

"What's the matter?" I asked almost bumping into her. She had stopped in the middle of the trail scouting ahead.

"I thought we'd be back before dark until this," she said. Ahead of us were dozens of giant pines, ripped from the rocky soil, roots and all, and they appeared tossed together like an armful of firewood dropped on the floor. Ahead of us was a tangled mess we had to travel through.

"Nolka was right. Blackfeather must have been pretty mad. Crawling over these big guys will take some time," Abby said.

"There's no way around this?" I asked.

"Not unless you're part mountain goat," she said looking at the cliffs on both sides. "I know I'm not feeling that way right now."

"Hey, see that cut down the canyon wall?" I asked. Off to our left was a crease in the face of the sheer wall, as if someone had taken a swipe with a knife down the side of a block of clay. "I bet we could find foot holds to climb that pretty easily, like the crevasse in the tunnel."

"I don't think so, Charlie. If we even made it to the top with these pack baskets, we have a different set of challenges. We'd have to find a place to climb back down, get the plants, and then climb back up again only to climb back down after all that. That's four climbs plus the hike up there. I don't want to take a chance, get hurt, and have our mission fail."

"Going along that ridge and doing all that climbing would take much longer," I agreed.

"Even if it were possible," Abby added.

We came to the first downed tree. It looked like a giant hand had roared into the canyon and pushed over everything higher than a few feet. This was going to be very hard going.

"How do you want to do this?" Abby asked.

"We can hand off packs," I offered. "You first?"

"Good idea," Abby agreed. Maybe we can use some of the limbs to climb up."

"And I could always give you ten to get you to reach one," I offered.

"Ten?" she asked.

"My ten fingers interlocked under your foot to give you a lift?" I explained.

"Oh. Of course," she replied. She had that serious look as if she had never heard the expression before but was reluctant to admit it. I put out my hands, fingers locked together.

"Wait, the packs," Abby warned. We shed our packs and I put out my hands again, fingers interlocked.

"Here you go," I said. She placed her foot in my hand, knee bent and her hand on my shoulder.

"I see a place to grab hold," Abby said.

"Okay, on three," I said. I paused.

"Okay," she replied.

"Ready, …. Three." Of course, Abby expected I would skip 'one' and 'two.' She straightened out her knee, grabbed the stub of a broken branch and in a blink was perched on the topside of the tree trunk, smiling down at me.

"Can't fool me, Charlie," she said.

"Just grab this, will you?" I asked, handing her pack basket up to her. "What do you have in here, rocks?" Her pack basket was much heavier than I thought it would be.

"There's only a little dried food in there, beef and a few beans. It shouldn't be that heavy for such a big boy. Hey, what would happen if we left some of these beans here?"

"Please, don't even think about it," I moaned. I found that I had no tolerance for time travel mind games.

"No, really, what bad things could happen?" Abby pestered.

"Well, maybe nothing," I said. "There might not be enough to make a difference. Hard saying', not knowin' Here," I said and handed up my pack. Abby balanced both baskets on the topside of the fallen tree while I climbed up.

"There is one thing that worries me, though," I said. "I've been having the dreams again."

"What?" she said, as she moved to make room beside her.

"The black wings have returned," I replied. I settled down, my hand steadying my pack Abby was holding for me while I climbed up.

"Why didn't you say something? You know what that means, and we agreed that you'd tell me if the dreams returned." Abby wasn't happy.

"I know, and I am telling you," I said, "but it was just the last two nights. I thought the dreams came from the stress of this trip."

"Every time you dream about Ki'kwa'jenu, he tends to show up, and I don't want him flying off with either one of us in his talons," Abby said as she looked around. "And that could happen! Who knows what spirit size differences there are here? I don't want to find out!"

"You're right," I said. "Sorry. I'll tell you the next time. It's the details of the dream that return to scare me."

"Those details are only going to be scary when we really get grabbed by sharp talons," Abby said. She reached out her hand and placed it over mine. "I have a confession to make, though."

"What could you possibly have to confess about?" I asked jokingly.

"I've been having the same dream the last two nights," she answered. "But it's not about anything bad, at least I don't think so."

"What happens?"

"My mother is standing, her back to me, and she's pointing to a path that leaves a clearing and enters dark woods. Just where the clearing and the woods meet, a young girl in native dress is walking away in the mist. I have no idea what it means," she said.

"At least they're not black wings stalking you," I replied.

Just then, a shadow passed over us. The hair on the back of my neck rose. It was not a cloudy day. We looked up to see a giant nighthawk sailing in circles above us, plunging us into darkness at each pass.

"Can you see the size of those talons?" I asked.

"And that beak?" was her reply.

"Quick! Let's get some cover. We'll come back for the packs." I screamed.

A bolt of lightning accompanied with an instant crack of thunder split the air. I was so startled that I almost missed my hand hold as we lowered ourselves to the log just below us. We looked up to see dark clouds rolling up the canyon. The wind began to rise, but this was from the north. Thunderstorms always came from the west. What was going on? Raindrops spurred by the north wind hit like needles on our upturned faces. Then the hail began.

"We'd better get under here fast," I said, and we crawled under another fallen tree leaning over our heads. We got to safety just in time as huge chunks of ice began battering the fallen log above us. I've seen hail before and never anything larger than a big blueberry, but these hail stones were as big as softballs. If any one of them hit us, it would really hurt, or worse.

"What would happen if the stream rose suddenly from a storm like this?" I shouted to Abby. The wind and now driving rain made it harder to hear.

"I don't care about the stream, it's those talons that worry me more!" She shouted back.

"We have to wait out the storm here," I told her. "These trees won't be going anywhere soon." Then the wind dropped off as suddenly as it had arrived. We climbed back up, shouldered our packs and began to move on.

Like a pair of foraging ants, we crawled over the fallen giants. I could see other downed trees ahead. We were able to climb around them using the limbs on each side like rungs of a ladder. We still had to hand off our packs. Having them on our backs wouldn't give us the space to pass in between the branches.

"Do you think that bird will come back?" Abby asked when we were taking a rest.

"It's Ki'kwa'jenu," I said quietly.

"Do you think he's looking for you?" Abby asked.

"He is much bigger in this time. I'm not so sure he saw us. Maybe at first, but we got under cover pretty fast," I said. "I'm hoping he's forgotten about me."

Hours passed. We navigated the maze of broken pine boughs and huge trunks scattered about. If anyone had been on this trail during the storm, they would not have survived. After a short descent down a field of boulders, we came again to the edge of the stream.

We walked along it for a short distance when we came to trees that looked like willows. All between the willows were the most beautiful colored foliage, as if fall had pushed spring and summer out of the way in that storm. Tiny red shoots, like whiskers, covered the leaves, giving them the illusion of velvet.

"Look, there they are!" Abby shouted. The leaves on these were much larger than we were expecting.

"Are these the right ones?" I asked. "Their leaves are so much bigger."

"Grandmother Molly said they were this size, but to be sure, let's check the drawings." Abby removed the oil cloth pack from her basket, unwrapped the covering and pulled out one of the sketches. "That's the one," she said. "These are the same shape, and the veins and edges are identical. Those red shoots are exactly what we should be looking for. We have to be careful to get most of the roots or the plant will wither to nothing before we get back."

Abby and I found several flat sticks, and we began to dig around the plants. The roots looked like large parsnips. They seemed to interlock with neighboring plants. As we began to dig them up, I thought I could smell licorice, and that was one of the identifiers Grandmother Molly told us to look for. There were many of them, and it didn't take long to fill each basket half-way, leaving room for the rest of our supplies we had stashed at the other side of Skull Cave. After washing our hands in the stream, we found our way back by following the same game path and climbing over the result of Kabibonokka's wrath. Or was it Blackfeather's wrath? I wondered if they were one in the same. When we were within sight of the village stockade, we paused to rest.

"We should head back to the cavern," Abby said. "Grandmother Molly's patients are waiting, and it's starting to get dark. We can make camp after we leave the tunnels and be back by tomorrow noon." We were staring at the stockade in the distance, watching residents come and go when I felt a hand on my shoulder.

"Hey, who are you?" I heard someone say. When I turned around, I saw a man dressed in deerskin. He looked like one of the braves that Blackfeather had been walking with while we were looking through the spy glass.

"What are you doing here, spying on our village?" the other one asked Abby. He didn't look too pleased. That they were on to us so fast made me think we were expected. No one had seen us. But something had. It had to be Ki'kwa'jenu.

"We're collecting plants," Abby explained as she pointed to her pack basket. He looked inside at the plants half-filling the pack.

"Let's go," the other one said, and we were almost dragged through the stockade's gate to the longhouse where we had seen Blackfeather come and go. Several villagers were staring at us as we passed by.

"Let go of me," Abby screamed at him, struggling to get away. He grabbed her long, auburn hair, and I got really mad.

"Let her go!" I shouted. The south wind began to rise, and soon a cloud of dust sailed across the yard like a miniature tornado. He let go of Abby's hair as we came to the long house. As soon as he did, the wind began to die back. I was so angry with them that I was afraid I was going to level the entire village. No one was going to hurt Abby! I could see fear in the eyes of the villagers who watched the spectacle.

Blackfeather walked to the long house and met us as we approached the barred door and spoke sharply to the two braves in his raspy voice.

"Put them inside, in the back room," he said. "I'll deal with them later," And he walked away. One took my arm, and another took Abby's. We were frog marched through the gate toward the long house where we saw Blackfeather exit. The guards unbarred the door and opened it. We were pushed inside, still wearing our packs, and dragged to the end of the long house and into a back room. When the door that separated the storage area from the rest of the longhouse closed, I could hear something being placed across it.

"What's he trying to accomplish by holding us prisoners?" I asked Abby.

"Not sure," she said, rubbing her shoulder. "We're no threat to them, but they must think so. They're pretty rough. That hurt! Even my hair aches!" Abby started rubbing her neck. "I'm glad you stopped the wind," she said.

"I was pretty mad. If I couldn't get my anger under control, the village would look like the trees in Kabibonokka's canyon."

"I figured that," Abby said.

A little light was filtering through the small gaps in the wall, and we could see some of the things stored inside. Besides the small hole at the top that let the smoke out, there was a window on each side, and there on the floor in the corner was a lumpy blanket. We could hear some rustling from whatever it covered.

"Who do you think that is?" I asked.

"Most likely it's Mahtagwaysoo," Abby suggested. The rustling stopped when her name was mentioned. A young woman stuck out her head.

"Is that you, Mahtagwaysoo?" I heard Abby ask while I was giving the back wall of the hut a good look. I found a place behind a tall basket where someone had already been digging a way out.

"Yes," a voice said.

"Are you alright?" Abby asked, helping her out from under the blanket. Mahtagwaysoo held a tomahawk in her left hand.

"I'm okay," was the reply. "He didn't hurt me. I snuck in here from the main room just to get away from him. I couldn't get out the front door because it was jammed tight. I've been trying to break through the back wall with this tomahawk I found. Where are you from? I haven't seen you before."

"We're visiting from another clan. We're friends of Nolka" Abby explained. Mahtagwaysoo seemed to accept the explanation. "Why are you hiding?" Abby asked. "This is Blackfeather's place, so won't he find you back here?"

"He probably knows I'm back here, but he hasn't come in back yet to drag me outside. I was hoping he had forgotten me for a bit. When he does show up, I'll be ready," she said. "I don't care what my father says. I'm not going to marry him!" She brandished the tomahawk, red ochre on the tasseled handle. Her hand, the same bloody color as the ochre stained anything that came in contact with it, looked like it had just committed murder. Younger than Abby, slender with strong cheekbones and fine eyebrows, Mahtagwaysoo's darting black eyes surveyed the room repeatedly.

"You have the same hair as Erik," she said.

"Erik?" Abby asked.

"His skin is like yours, too. He's from a different clan on the big water where the rivers meet." Mahtagwaysoo was describing where the Penobscot meets the sea. I hadn't thought about Viking visits, but this was some compelling evidence.

Blackfeather's lodge was big, and this back room was no exception. There was a ton of stuff stored here. Tall baskets were everywhere, and most were large enough for a person to hide in. I'm sure they were full of grains and dried fish. There were piles of colorful blankets and dozens of untipped spear shafts leaning against the wall. Cured skins from moose, deer and bear were in piles here and there. Blackfeather had collected a lot of valuable furs. These were probably gifts from the successful hunting parties he directed.

The daylight was now gone, now a time of mystery when shadows around the trees could be anything at all. From a small opening in the side of the longhouse, I could see a glow from the courtyard. Men were adding logs to a large bonfire. Several were wearing headdresses of different designs. Others wore a group of feathers behind a band with other smaller ones dangling below it. All had painted faces of red, white and black, that made them look like fierce warriors.

"What are we going to do?" I asked Abby.

"We have to escape," she said. Then in a whisper that only I could hear, "We need to get back to the cavern and make the jump back to our own time before Blackfeather finds out we're gone."

"I've been working on the back wall," Mahtagwaysoo told us.

"If you move that third basket from the left, you'll see where I've been digging."

Although the sun had not set, we heard drumming coming from around the fire. Through some small gaps in the hut's wall, we could see several people dancing around the flames. It was a slow dance at first, but soon the beat picked up, and the chants became louder. *We really need to get out of this hut before they come for us*, I thought. *And they will come for us.*

The back wall was not well made. I moved the basket aside and found where Mahtagwaysoo had been trying to loosen the upright poles. I thought we might be able to push through. Using the stone knife on my belt, I was able free some of the wall support stuck in the ground. Sometimes a prison is more in the mind of the prisoner, when freedom is on the other side of an unlocked door. I kept at it, and soon I was able to dislodge and then spread apart two of the supporting poles when the sound of the main door to the longhouse being unfastened warned me to cover up my little escape effort by sliding the tall basket back to its place. Soon, we heard the bar across the door to the storage room being removed. When the door opened, I was innocently sitting with Abby. Mahtagwaysoo was standing by the doorway with her tomahawk held high, expecting to bop Blackfeather a good one. He'd get a surprise when he waltzed in to drag her to the marriage ceremony. Our visitor was tall and backlit by both the full moon rising over the old village and the bonfire in the courtyard. We couldn't make out a face at first. Mahtagwaysoo waited behind the door with her tomahawk raised.

Nodumkanwet
(Serpent Spirit)
Chapter 13

Wearing traditional deerskin tasseled clothing, a tall figure with dark hair flowing over her shoulders came through the entrance. She carried herself like royalty, a straight back and head held high. It was Running Deer.

"Nolka!" Abby exclaimed, looking at our visitor. Nolka put her finger to her lips, then looked back over her shoulder, then closed the door behind her while checking to see if anyone had followed her into the longhouse. There were no signs of any guards. I think everyone was dancing around the fire by now. Nolka must have seen us being herded inside.

"It is not safe for you to remain here. You must return to the cavern and your own clan," Nolka said. "Most are at the feast of the hunters, and this place is not guarded right now. If you come with me, I can lead you to the trail that will take you back to the cavern. Quickly, before Blackfeather brings you to the feast."

"And makes me marry him!" Mahtagwaysoo cried, waving her weapon.

"I've made an opening in the back," I said. "We're almost ready to go now."

In seconds, we had the poles apart a bit more and were about to slither outside with our pack baskets when Nolka stopped us and pointed to Mahtagwaysoo, who was standing right behind her, a white knuckled grip on the tomahawk.

"You must take her with you," said Nolka. "The marriage ceremony will take place at tonight's feast. Soon, the women will come in to dress her. She has to get away now, and she has nowhere to go!"

I wondered how moving her from one time to another far in the future would affect everything else. She was young and didn't have a family. Only Grandmother Molly would know for sure, but we couldn't just ring her up on the village phone to ask. Hiram didn't want us to bring anything modern when we stepped out of the cave, but he didn't say anything about bringing something back. We were bringing back plants, but a person as well? Not what we had planned. I was a little nervous.

"Should she really come with us?" I asked.

"We don't have time to argue this," Abby said. "She's coming. We act first, and ask for forgiveness after, okay?" I nodded my head and dropped to the floor to squeeze through the narrow opening in the wall. I reached back inside for the two baskets.

"I hope she's called Little Rabbit for a good reason," I replied. "She'd better move fast!" I pulled the baskets through and then waited behind a large tree in back of the hut for the others. Mahtagwaysoo came next followed by Abby. Nolka stayed behind to cover up the escape route, and went out through the front, barring both doors behind her as she left. Nolka casually walked around the longhouse, checking to see if anyone noticed her before ducking behind it. Soon, she joined us.

It was early evening now, and the full moon had released the path from the shadows that strangled the woods. Mahtagwaysoo, Nolka, Abby and I hid behind some trees while we figured out the safest route to the cavern. We had a good view of the feast and the ceremonial dancing that was snaking around a tall totem pole and a large bonfire.

"Come on, Abby, we have to get out of here," I said. "They could come for us anytime."

"In a minute," she replied. 'I want to see this. Look at the top of the totem pole!"

"That's a big totem," I observed. Black wings protruded from each side of the very top. "It has to be a symbol of Ki'kwa'jenu."

While we watched from the safety of the pines, a costumed figure came from the darkness beyond the fire. Its head and body were covered in green scales, and its mouth was full of long, sharp teeth.

I had heard of this evil spirit, the Nodumkanwet. The figure danced around the fire, brandishing a spear at anyone who came close. Then, dressed in the costume of an owl, another figure came into the firelight and began to chase the scaly beast around the fire to the howls of those who watched. The owl pushed a fake spear toward the Nodumkanwet's side, and the scaly beast fell to the ground, wriggling like a fish. When the movement ceased, the mock battle was over. The actor took off the owl mask. This was one of Blackfeather's buddies who had dragged us into the longhouse. He stood, howling his victory, one foot on the vanquished foe's chest and his hand on the spear that was now wedged in the ground beside the Nodumkanwet. The tribe cheered. The owl stood up, and the two costumed actors disappeared into the shadows. The first act had ended.

The drumming continued, softer and then louder as if a spirit was being summoned. Soon, a dark figure appeared at the edge of the clearing, staying just at the border between shadows and firelight.

"Okay, I've seen enough," Abby said. "Let's go," and she turned to leave.

"Wait, Abby, look at the wings," I whispered. I think I stopped breathing. Abby turned back to see.

"We have to go, Charlie!" she said. "They're going to come for us soon!"

"Not yet. I think Ki'kwa'jenu is making an appearance, and I have to see it," I said. It was more dangerous to keep watching, but I felt compelled to stay.

A dark figure circled the open area. I could see its bright red eyes, like glassy stones reflecting the light, a yellow beak and spreading, giant black wings. Ki'kwa'jenu came into the full light of the bonfire. Lifting its long, black talons, the Nighthawk darted towards those standing nearby, scattering screaming observers into the shadows, then retreating back to the firelight. The actor repeated this mock attack several times as he made his way around the circle of observers.

When he charged into the crowd, Ki'kwa'jenu wrapped his wings like human arms around a young boy, dragging the screaming child from his parents. Spectators watched in horror. Was this what had happened to the missing girls? By the time Ki'kwa'jenu had pulled the boy away from the crowd, the owl re-emerged from the shadows and came after them. In the struggle, Ki'kwa'jenu tried to wrestle the owl to the ground, still dragging the frightened child away toward the fire. Shouts came from the crowd while the two predators fought over the victim. The boy's screams became louder. I stood still, barely able to breathe. It was real for the child. It became real to me as I could see one of my nightmares playing out before me. Ki'kwa'jenu kept a tight grip on the boy who was now screaming even louder while the crowd began to roar in anger.

The owl began to stir. It rose to its feet and to the cheers of everyone. It flapped its wings, going straight to the distressed child. The owl came between the black wings and the boy, freeing him to run to his parents who wrapped him in their arms and stepped back from the light.

"That looked too real," Abby said.

"I think that's the point. I wouldn't want that boy's dreams tonight," I replied. "Mine are bad enough!"

The owl began to thrash Ki'kwa'jenu' with its wings while the Nighthawk screeched. Ki'kwa'jenu fought back, the two figures coming at each other, retreating, and coming to blows again, gray and black feathers drifting in the still night air. When they were in the middle of the circle of light the owl held something out to Ki'kwa'jenu'. The owl was chanting.

"What is he saying?" I asked Abby. "I can't make out the words." "He's casting a spell," she said. "Look at what's in the owl's hand." Seeming to glow in the red and orange firelight, a large piece of yellow quartz caught everyone's attention. The owl thrust it into Ki'kwa'jenu who then collapsed in a heap of blackness. Its eyes seemed to stop glowing. The owl did a victory dance about the still figure, facing the cheering crowd while turning its back on the fallen foe. The victory was short lived.

Ki'kwa'jenu began to move and stood up. The crowd began to shout warnings to the owl, but it seemed not to hear them. Ki'kwa'jenu attacked from behind, wrapping its huge black wings around the surprised owl who went limp and fell to the ground, not moving. The gasps from the crowd told me how stunned they were. From everyone's reaction, it looked like this was the first time this part of the struggle had been acted out. His red eyes glowing again, Ki'kwa'jenu danced to the faster beats until the drums stopped. Ki'kwa'jenu pulled the quartz charm from his feathers and pretended to swallow it. Spreading its wings, red eyes aglow, it danced around the fire one more time before standing still. The Ki'kwa'jenu figure then removed its mask. There stood Blackfeather with a menacing grin, holding high the crystal of yellow quartz that glowed from the same orange firelight that illuminated all our faces.

"Spells and crystals don't seem to work with Ki'kwa'jenu," I whispered.

"Not those at least," sighed Abby.

"He's become a threat to our clan," came a soft voice from behind us. We turned to face a man with young Moosis by his side. His kind face seemed familiar with many of Molly's features, eyes and strong cheekbones just like hers. His once black hair was now mixed with silver, tied in a ponytail secured with a carved ivory clasp that must have come from far away after many trades, just as Molly described. It was Gray Wolf.

"Awasosqua is well?" he asked. His voice had a calming tone to it.

"Yes, she is well. Awasosqua is my grandmother," Abby told him. I wondered how he knew we had come from her time. "She gives you her love and thanks." Gray Wolf smiled.

"Please tell Awasosqua we miss her," Nolka said.

"How did you know who I was?" Abby asked him.

"Not many have the fiery hair from the Lynx Clan," he said. "I knew who you were when I saw what was around your neck," as he pointed to the amulet. "How is my daughter?"

"She is well and wants you to know she is grateful for protecting her the way you did. She also wants to know she loves you very much and misses you." I could see that Abby was struggling with the last sentence, a hitch or two in her voice.

"Tell her we are glad she has a good life, but wish she were with us. Why has she sent you?" Gray Wolf asked.

"There is a sickness in her clan, and we came here to harvest the plant to cure it," Abby explained. "It no longer grows in our time."

"I imagine there are other changes, aren't there?" Gray Wolf asked.

"Hunting isn't as good, and neither is the fishing, but we all get by okay," Abby replied. "Life is a little different, and time seems to move much faster."

"Hunting has been very good here lately," Gray Wolf replied. "But I'm afraid it's come at a high cost. Blackfeather is a dangerous man and must be stopped. It will take more than a courageous person to do it."

"Don't others support him because he knows where the game is?" Abby asked.

"Yes, that's true. He's gathered a pretty good following," Gray Wolf said. "There's not much to be done about it. Most of the clan supports him, but those who do, do so in fear. I see that you have Mahtagwaysoo with you."

"They got me out of that little prison of his," Mahtagwaysoo said. "I can't wait to give him a few blows with this," as she held the stone club in front of her, shaking it. "He can't be allowed to get away with this behavior."

"He'll get what he deserves," Gray Wolf said, "and I hope that happens soon. Moosis and I have to get back, or we will be missed." He put his hand on Moosis' shoulder and looked our way as he turned. "Travel safely, and give my love to Awasosqua." And they turned and walked back into the crowd.

I was watching for the guards to return. The drumming and chanting had become much louder. How much longer before they come for us? I wondered.

"I could hide behind a tree and give him a blow on the back of his head with this when he passes by," Mahtagwaysoo said, holding up the club.

"And if his buddies caught you?" Abby asked. "There'd be nothing left after they finished with you."

"I'll give them a good fight," she said, waving the weapon with determination. She looked pretty angry, and I wouldn't want to cross her.

Come on," I said. "They're going to be looking for us soon. We have to go, and right now."

Nolka pointed to the dome where the cavern was located. "It's up there," she said.

The bright moonlight made it easy to see the path. We crept through the woods, Nolka guiding us to the trail that led to the cavern. When we could see the path clearly, Nolka stopped, reached out and hugged Abby. The smile on Nolka's face told us how happy she was to have saved Mahtagwaysoo who was looking over her shoulder while keeping a white-knuckle grip on the stone club.

"*Oleohneh*," Nolka said. "*Olibamkanny*."

"What?" I asked, turning to Abby who brought up the rear. I had a hard time understanding Nolka's accent.

"She said, 'Thank you,' and 'Travel well', I think." The drumming stopped, and we could hear yells in the distance.

If the moonlight made the trail easy for us to see, then any pursuers would have no problem following us. I led the way followed by Mahtagwaysoo, and Abby followed right behind.

"Shouldn't Mahtagwaysoo be told about where we're going?" I asked Abby. "She might be a bit confused when we get back."

I stopped climbing and waited for Mahtagwaysoo and Abby to catch up.

Abby turned to Mahtagwaysoo. "We're going to travel many summers from here," Abby told her.

"From now?" Mahtagwaysoo asked, her brow furrowed.

"Yes, from now." Abby looked at her closely, trying to read her reaction.

"How many summers?" she asked.

"More than we can count in a day's time," Abby replied. "Many things will be different, too."

"How?" she asked.

"You'll see, said Abby. "We don't have time to talk about it now. We've got to keep going. I think they're coming."

The voices behind us were getting louder. We were halfway up the steep trail when Blackfeather's goons caught up to us. I was giving Mahtagwaysoo a boost over a large boulder. Abby was a few steps behind us, starting to climb over a tree trunk fallen across the path. A figure from below reached out for Abby's legs. The raven feathers on his headband told me who it was. I could taste fear, but at the same time my rage began to boil. I pushed Mahtagwaysoo ahead of me, pointing to the alder bushes that masked the cave's entrance, the wind rising from the south.

"Go now! Wait at the tunnel!" I said. She nodded and started to climb over the boulders. I was worried she'd come after Blackfeather and get recaptured.

I heard Abby scream.

"Charlie!" she yelled. "Help me! He's got my leg!"

"I'm coming," I yelled back. I looked at Mahtagwaysoo who was standing still and motioned for her to keep climbing. Then I turned around and took a few steps back to find Abby, her left leg now in the strong grip of Blackfeather's giant hand. Abby was holding on to a tree root with both hands and kicking dirt down on him with the other foot. I grabbed for her forearm and she reached for mine. Abby was being pulled from both directions, and Blackfeather seemed to be winning.

"Charlie!" she shouted. "My hand is starting to slip." Out of nowhere and under a clear sky, the south wind rose to a gale. I heard a tree crack. A splintered oak branch came crashing down over Blackfeather, pinning him on the ground, his grip releasing her ankle. While I was pulling Abby toward me, Mahtagwaysoo had climbed back down to us. Sliding just below Abby, she whacked Blackfeather' still outstretched arm with her weapon, not once, but twice. He howled in pain. Another wind began to rise from the north.

He howled and let go of Abby's foot. I could hear Blackfeather's shouts piercing the forest while we climbed up to the cave entrance. The wind was now howling when we entered the cave. It had been a while since I had been angry enough to summon Sowanakik, but this wasn't Sowanakik. This was Kabibonokka. Blackfeather could summon the wind, but from the opposite direction! I could see his goons cowering behind the trees for protection from the suddenly reversed gale. Two were brave enough to run to Blackfeather as he cradled his injured arm, his helpers trying to pull away the oak branch blocking their ascent.

We walked toward the opening of the tunnel. There was a little shelf just before it. I was following Abby and could see her limping. "Are you okay?"

"I'm fine," Abby said. "I just twisted my ankle a little when I was being pulled apart." She kept limping on. I tapped her right shoulder. She stopped and turned to me. "It would not have been good if Blackfeather had won that tug-of-war," she quipped. "Thanks for saving me. By the look on his face, I wouldn't have lasted long if he got me."

I was really worried about you," I confessed, "and I could really use a hug right now." Abby gave me a real bear hug and I squeezed back. I felt better right away. She turned around to take a step, so when I needed to wipe away a tear, I turned over my shoulder to see how far ahead of us Little Rabbit was. I could barely see who it was scurrying over the boulders ahead of us as we got closer to the opening of the tunnel.

"Hey, Mahtagwaysoo," I shouted. She turned. "Wait up!" She sat down, took off her moccasins and began to soak her feet in the ice-cold water trickling down between clean washed boulders of the ancient riverbed.

"We need to catch up with little Rabbit," I said. "Can you make it to the cavern alright?" I asked. Abby stopped and turned.

"Not so fast," she demanded. "What's that wet spot on your cheek?"

"Okay, okay, I'm just a softie when it comes to you," I grinned. "Now, let's get going."

I looked back at the trail we had climbed, and there were two men hanging around the first little rise, watching us, most likely deciding what to do next.

When we entered the tunnel, I lit the torch we had left there earlier and handed it to Abby who led the way with Mahtagwaysoo between us, still holding her weapon, sputtering curses against Blackfeather. We walked into the darkness. I prayed we didn't meet up with any bears or black wings.

Sowanakik
(South Wind)
Chapter 14

We found our way through the tunnel and back into the large cavern. Mahtagwaysoo kept an iron grip on her club as she looked behind us. Our moccasins made no sound. It was quiet from all directions except for the plinks of a little water dripping down one of the glassy sides of the tunnel. We came into the cavern. The small opening would let a little light in, but it was night now. We needed the torch to see the stone altar before us.

Abby took the amulet from around her neck and showed it to Mahtagwaysoo. "We'll be out of here soon," Abby said to her in a calm, confidant voice.

Abby beckoned us to stand beside her at the altar. After she placed the amulet in the round depression that seemed to have been made for it, Abby looked at me.

"I don't know if this will work for three."

"I hope it does," I said, "and you'd better hurry up. I hear voices coming down the tunnel. Look, there's the reflection of a torch."

I could see a yellow light dancing along the wet sides of the smooth cave walls. Abby began her chant, and we held hands in a chain, first Abby at the altar, then me, and last Mahtagwaysoo. Molly warned us that when there was more than one traveler, we had to be in physical contact with one another or just the person touching the amulet would make the journey.

We could hear shouting from where the tunnel entered the cavern. I recognized one voice; it was Blackfeather's. Three warriors walked into the cavern, two with spears in hand. The third held his bow drawn, the arrow tipped with a white quartz arrowhead ready to fly. Blackfeather led the pack, still cradling his injured arm.

I was hoping we'd arrive in the right time and place. Our first two tries were a bit shaky, and we didn't want to make a mistake and have to come back here when these guys might be waiting for us. Abby was nearly finished with the ritual when the men took a few more steps closer, now shouting at us. Mahtagwaysoo shouted back, using words Olive had not taught us. She was spitting mad.

Just when Abby was speaking the last of the ritual, Blackfeather lunged forward to grab Mahtagwaysoo. With her free arm, she swung the club at his head, arcing through the air where his skull had just been as he and his companions faded away like the morning mist, their voices getting fainter and fainter, vanishing into the shadows of past time.

"That was close!" I said. "He almost came with us."

"That would be bad, and he nearly got killed too," Abby said. "We already have one problem with Mahtagwaysoo and don't need another with Blackfeather." Mahtagwaysoo was now out of time. Everything she did would affect things from this point on. That couldn't be changed, but she could be brought back if Grandmother Molly thought we needed to make the trip again. I hoped she wouldn't need any more plants.

"As soon as we get out of this cavern, we'll feel a lot better in the fresh air," I said.

Abby nodded her head, "Okay, let's go and find out when we are." Abby stood still.

"What's the matter?" I asked.

"Which tunnel?" she said. "We have to go out the one we were supposed to come in through, but which is it?" Before us were several openings. We had bypassed the one we were supposed to use, but nothing bad happened as a result.

"I know the way," Mahtagwaysoo said from behind us. "My grandfather was a shaman who took me here many times. I remember what he told me about the tunnels. He never explained why, but he told me it was important to leave the cavern only through those two, the one we came in through, and that one over there." She pointed to a tunnel not quite opposite of the one we just used. "I remember a big waterfall on the other side. We had to walk under it. Sometimes braves from nearby clans come there to get flint for their arrowheads and knives." Abby and I looked at each other and then smiled at her, nodding our heads.

"Let's go," Abby said. "You lead the way."

Mahtagwaysoo took the torch and led us out. Moving through thirty-five centuries was unsettling. Or did we really make that trip? We wouldn't be sure we had ended up in the right time until we retraced our steps back to Split Rock and then on to Grandmother Molly's village. Even then, we could be in a different time stream.

"Abby," I said. She was in front of me. I could see the glow of Mahtagwaysoo's torch.

"What?"

"Does Mahtagwaysoo know about the bear and the escape route we had to take?"

"No," she said. She cried out to Mahtagwaysoo, who stopped. When we caught up to her, Abby explained about the bear. The light from the torch glowed off the smooth tunnel walls as if to make things even brighter. Ahead, I could see the opening in the ceiling we had to use for an escape route on the trip in.

"Come on, let's get out of this tunnel and past the waterfall," Abby said. Mahtagwaysoo continued to lead through the tunnel. Just as we got to the spot just under the ceiling opening there was a blur of motion as the bear got up and roared at us while she stood on her hind legs. The hair rose on the back of my neck as Mahtagwaysoo lunged the torch at the howling beast, driving it back, then on the run with her three little cubs ahead and behind her.

"Why didn't we think of that?" I asked.

"We kind of did, but we weren't brave enough to hold on to the torch, I guess." Abby smiled at Mahtagwaysoo.

"Seeing that bear again was scary, but it's a good sign that we're in the right time," I said.

"I'm pretty glad we brought her back," Abby said.

We passed behind the waterfall. Mahtagwaysoo led us across the slippery rocks and flat ledge that had water seeping over it. Above us was a curved arch of stone with veins of different colors. Some had been quarried for stone tools. None of the quarry sites were recent. That was another good sign, I thought.

Everything I saw looked much the same when we left. The mill was belching smoke and steam. In the distance the trees looked about right, and the silver threads of the rivers clogged with pulpwood suggested we were in the right time, too.

After we found our way outside, we located the food cache and repacked our baskets one more time. I was happy to have the rifle with me again. We put our arms through the backpack straps and cinched them tight for the trip back to the campsite. Mahtagwaysoo's eyes were pretty wide when she first saw the rifle, then the lights of the town and the mill in the distance.

"Where's the village?" she asked in surprise. "Where did it go?"

"It no longer exists in our time," Abby told her. "What you see below us is a place that makes paper and the long houses where people live."

"Paper?" Mahtagwaysoo said.

"Something to draw a map on," Abby said. "Like birch bark." Mahtagwaysoo didn't seem impressed.

"The air smells," she said, "Really bad!" Little Rabbit spit several times as if to clear her mouth of an unpleasant taste. "Why are there so many fireflies below in their paper village?" There were lots of homes lit up by electric lights, streetlights outlining grids of housing developments around the mill.

"Those are like torches that people use to see their way at night," I offered.

"The trees are so much shorter," she said. "And why don't any grow in some places?" Mahtagwaysoo was scowling at the patchwork quilt of clear cut where all the trees had been mowed down like hay in a farmer's field.

Mahtagwaysoo now followed Abby, and I followed her. It was hard going, and this time my feet were really getting sore in the thin moccasins I was wearing. A sudden shower made the trip harder. The trail became slippery, and in some places, it had disappeared under rivulets. Part way down the boulder field, we crawled under a tarp and changed into heavier boots and decent socks. Mahtagwaysoo was only mildly curious about the tarp and our change in footwear. It wasn't long before the rain stopped, the sky cleared, and we continued on to Nicatou. The moon lit our way. We walked across the little ledge, holding on to the branches of mountain ash that grew from crevasses all around us. In September, there would be yellow-orange berries that fermented after the first frost, making them a tasty bear treat. A drunk bear wasn't the safest animal to be around! We climbed down boulders to a little beach beside the stream. There, in the high grass, was a level spot for the tent. Abby made a campfire while Mahtagwaysoo gathered firewood and I got out the food.

We pitched the tent. It was big enough for the three of us. We had an extra blanket that Mahtagwaysoo wrapped herself in.

"Where are we going?" Mahtagwaysoo asked.

"To Awasosqua's village," Abby said. "At Nicatou. You'll be safe there, but we have to be sure it's okay that you're here with us. Grandmother will decide."

"I don't like it here. I'd rather beat up Blackfeather!" Mahtagwaysoo said. "The water is different, the air stinks, there are fewer trees and most aren't very tall. How can you live here?"

"A lot has changed," I explained. "It's been many seasons since leaving your village, but most changes are recent. Money and the Company have done all this." I waved my hand across the scene. I found myself becoming more and more angry at just what had been done to the world we lived in. A pristine country had been turned into a festering garbage dump. The more I thought of the damage, the angrier I became.

The wind began to rise, and soon the ashes of our campfire were blowing into our tent.

"Will you let Sowanakik have a rest?" Abby screamed at me over the roar of the wind I had summoned in my anger. "It doesn't help us right now! And there're ashes everywhere in here!" Abby shouted as she brushed the ashes away from her bedroll. In a moment, the wind calmed as I began to relax. We began to brush things off.

Mahtagwaysoo's eyes widened. "Sowanakik?" she said.

"Yes," I replied. "Only when I get angry. Sometimes Abby has to calm me down."

"And if she's not there?" Mahtagwaysoo asked.

"Then really bad things can happen," I said, remembering the men who had drowned the summer before when I tried to defend our family from mobsters. This time, man's avarice really got me steamed.

"We need to get our rest. We have to make it to Grandmother Molly's village tomorrow. People are dying." We wrapped up in our blankets, and we slept until dawn.

Nicatou
(The Rivers Join)
Chapter 15

We woke to a warm spring morning. The sun's rays poked through the spruce branches overhead as it rose over the low mountains in the East. A little mist swirled up through the needles, and the black flies were coming out. When the sun was the highest, the flies were more tolerable, but early mornings and evenings were the worst. I built a little fire, and Abby and Mahtagwaysoo found some fresh water and a few early strawberries. She had her first cup of coffee, but she didn't like it much, and had a mug of tea instead. I warmed up some beans, and Abby used the reflector oven to make some biscuits.

While we were eating, Abby expressed her concern about our guest.

"We have to ask Grandmother Molly what to do about Mahtagwaysoo," I said. We have no idea what we've messed up by bringing her with us. Who knows what problems her presence here will bring?"

"Grandmother Molly will know what has to be done if there's a problem. Maybe we won't have to return her to her own time. What's the matter, Charlie? You look worried."

"I promised I'd tell you when I saw them again," I said

"Saw what? Oh, don't tell me...you had a dream about Ki'kwa'jenu?" Abby asked. Before I could reply, Mahtagwaysoo

121

jumped up from the log bench by the fire pit.

"Ki'kwa'jenu!?!" she exclaimed. "You have seen the Nighthawk?" she asked as s picked up her tomahawk, coming closer, her forehead furrowed with concern and fear in her eyes.

Abby and I looked at each other. I thought Little Rabbit was going to bean me with her weapon, and I stepped back.

"Charlie Bear Claw dreams of the wings," Abby explained to her, holding out her hand to stop her forward motion. "The Nighthawk has left us alone, but still follows us day and night. It seems that only Charlie can see him."

"He wants your power, Charlie Bear Claw," Mahtagwaysoo said. "That is what he always comes for." Her dark eyes pivoted from one side to the other as if the Nighthawk was going to leap out from behind a tree. "He wants your bones for his nest, too."

"We know, Mahtagwaysoo. Ki'kwa'jenu has been following Charlie for some time now. If it were Charlie Bear Claw's power it wanted, the Nighthawk would take it, and Charlie would be gone," Abby told her. "You have to understand that Ki'kwa'jenu has less power in our time than he has in your time," Abby added.

Mahtagwaysoo seemed satisfied with Abby's explanation, yet we all kept looking over our shoulders, expecting the Nighthawk to jump out at us from the shadows.

"We'd better get going," Abby said. We packed up the tent, our bedrolls and the kitchen. I doused the campfire.

Abby hoisted her pack, turning to the trail. "Those thunderheads don't look too friendly," she observed. Off to the west, huge billows of white and black clouds were growing fast for early morning.

"Seems like bad weather likes to follow us along the river," I said.

"And black wings, too," Abby quipped, looking around for signs of the Nighthawk. When I looked back, I imagined I could see a pair of black wings following us in and out of the threatening clouds. *Are they really there?* I wondered.

....

I could tell we were getting closer to Split Rock by the grade of the trail. We were starting to climb, and soon we forded a little stream I recognized we had crossed on the way in. *Another good sign: it looks just the same,* I thought. *Now if that raven's nest was there, I'd be convinced we made it all the way back to the right time.* Sure enough, when we got close to the rocks, I could see the huge nest at the top of one of the cedars. Bits of glass were shining from the layers of twigs near the nest's side. I was relieved. This was a positive sign that nothing had changed since we left, and we had returned to the right time. We couldn't be certain until we saw Grandmother Molly and Hiram. Even then, with Abby's track record of landing us in the wrong time stream, there could still be something wrong in a major way that we haven't yet seen.

When we reached Nicatou Stream, we uncovered our canoe from the brush. The paddles and poles were right where we had left them. Those who needed a way across a pond or stream often swapped canoes, but ours had not been touched.

After we loaded up, we sat Mahtagwaysoo in the middle. I took the bow, and Abby took the stern. It was a balancing act since both Abby and I had to stand to use the poles. Pushing a canoe against the current with twelve-foot poles is never easy. Our passenger gave the canoe more stability with her added weight and a little more paddle power.

Mahtagwaysoo took a moment to look over the paddle just like she did the canoe. I'd forgotten she had never seen a canvas covered, cedar strip craft fastened with brass nails and covered in paint.

"Where are the eyes?" she asked. She meant the eyes usually drawn on the front of the canoe. 'How can it see where to go?"

"It's okay, we know the route," Abby said.

"You might, but the canoe doesn't," Mahtagwaysoo quipped. Abby sighed. Culture shock was difficult. Time travel didn't help.

We paddled our way across the current to Grandmother Molly's village.

We pulled up to the shore, unloaded and stashed the canoe, poles and paddles, grabbed our packs and started the last leg of the journey to the village. When we came into the clearing, we could see there were fewer people around.

We walked the path to Grandmother Molly's cabin where we found her in the rocking chair on her front porch. She had a fir branch in her hand, swatting away the black flies. It looked like she had been expecting us. A pitcher of lemonade and two glasses were on a tray on top of the little table beside her. But she hadn't been expecting all of us.

"What took you so long?" she asked, smiling. Then she saw Mahtagwaysoo behind me. The smile left her face. "And who might this be?"

"Meet Mahtagwaysoo," Abby said. She was hiding where we were imprisoned. Blackfeather was about to take her for his bride."

Grandmother Molly's face was unreadable, studying Mahtagwaysoo.

"I am Awasosqua," Grandmother Molly told her in the old language. "You must remember a young woman, Gray Wolf's daughter."

"But you're an old lady!" Little Rabbit exclaimed. Grandmother Molly burst out laughing.

"I sure am," she replied, "but when you knew me, I was very young. You remember playing together? You must understand that time passes differently, depending on your perspective. I truly am over seventy. You have come to me like a fish plucked out of the river." Little Rabbit was nodding a little. She was beginning to understand about the flow of time.

"Eagle Feather has your father's amulet?" she asked, looking at Abby.

"Yes, she does," Awasosqua replied. "For protection from Black Feather."

"Some of us weren't so lucky," Mahtagwaysoo quipped. "We still have not found the missing three." Grandmother Molly nodded. There was silence for a moment.

"We have the plants," said Abby, shrugging off her pack. I did the same. We had repacked the gear at the bottom so the plants would not be crushed. Grandmother Molly bent over each pack and selected one.

"You did well. I have not seen this plant for a long time, and never around here. Maybe the spirits will help some grow here now that we have some roots. I must prepare them. The black flies are really bad now. Let's move inside. We will talk while I work." Molly waved to the door. "Just take in this tray. I'll be right in with Mahtagwaysoo."

While Abby and I were pouring the lemonade, I could hear Grandmother Molly talking with Little Rabbit. Mahtagwaysoo was not happy about leaving her village. Soon, they came inside.

"Mahtagwaysoo told me she wants to go home," said Grandmother Molly. "She's convinced herself that she can beat up Blackfeather. What's that all about? What happened?"

Abby told her about finding Nolka, gathering the plants, our capture, her father's message, and the escape with Mahtagwaysoo as Blackfeather nearly recaptured us.

"Charlie brought up a big wind that brought down an oak branch on top of Blackfeather. Then Little Rabbit nailed his arm with her tomahawk. That slowed him down, and it gave us a chance to get away. We made it to the cavern, and we were at the altar. Charlie was holding one of my hands while he held Mahtagwaysoo's. As I finished with the ritual, Blackfeather and his goons burst into the cavern. As Blackfeather reached out for Mahtagwaysoo's arm, we disappeared. It was pretty close. He almost came with us."

"It's a good thing he didn't come here," said Grandmother Molly.

"They just faded away as we left the cavern," said Abby. "I don't think Mahtagwaysoo completely understands why her village seems to have disappeared.

"You mean the paper mill built where the long houses used to be?" I asked. "Who could possibly be upset by that?" I quipped. Father wasn't the only one who made deals with the Devil.

"She has to go back," Grandmother Molly said to us. "I've already seen changes here. One family has just disappeared."

"Who disappeared?" Abby asked.

"Remember the Mitchell Farm where they bought and sold horses?"

"Yeah, we walked right by it just before we left," I said. "Where do you think they went?" I asked.

"They never were. The parents aren't there, the whole family is gone along with all signs of a farm even being there. It's just forest. No field. I think the Mitchell's are direct descendants of Mahtagwaysoo. It's a good thing she wants to go back," she said.

The Return
Chapter 16

"What happens if we get locked up again?" I asked while trying not to sound too worried.

"Then we get locked up," Abby replied. "They don't have iron bars, and I didn't see any stone walled cells. We can get through any wall they make. We weren't searched last time, so we'll be okay if we get 'locked up.'"

"You don't seem too concerned," I observed. "I guess I worry too much." I reached for my coat hanging from a wooden peg on Molly's back porch, wondering how long it would take for my pen knife to cut through a four-inch thick log. If the penknife wasn't taken away, that is.

I took my coat off the peg to feel Abby put her arms around me from behind and rested her face between my shoulder blades. "It's a good thing you worry," she said, squeezing her arms around me. "You're the sane person who keeps me from doing crazy things."

"I guess I'm not doing a very good job of that," I said turning around. "Your little jaunt up the log jam plus what we're now going to do and where we're going. I doubt there'd be anything I could say to keep you here." Abby smiled at me.

"You're right about that," she said. "Mahtagwaysoo has to go back at least."

In conversations with Molly, it was clear that Mahtagwaysoo

wanted to go home. She didn't like how the air smelled or the construction of a large town on her village site. I can't say I blame her. The more important issue was how her absence from then affected now. An entire family and their descendants would cease to exist.

When we headed back to the petroglyphs, it was a calm, sunny day. The hike to Split Rock and then to the cavern was an anxious one for me. I kept looking over my shoulder for Ki'kwa'jenu. There was something about those black wings that spooked me. I never knew when they'd show up. We zipped along the path in back of the waterfall and through a recently vacated bear den.

Abby stood in front of the altar in the center of the domed cavern. The light from the opening above shone directly on the stone circle. I could see the petroglyphs and the carved outlines of feet where Abby stood. Abby reached for my hand. I reached for Mahtagwaysoo. After Abby finished the ritual, we still had no indication we were successful. We'd have to get outside to take a look at the surroundings to be sure.

It was pitch black inside the tunnels that connected to the main cavern. This time we had three torches with us. As we disappeared down a wet stone encased hall of mirrors, torchlights reflecting off glassy smooth yet faceted walls, I noticed a familiar, musk-ox smell. Then, some of the blackness started to move. A huge black bear stood on its hind legs and roared so loud my ears rang and rang. The bear's guttural cries pushed us back into Mahtagwaysoo, who had been following me closely. The bear roared at us, walking on back legs now, towering over us with its head nearly touching the tunnel's high ceiling. This beast was much larger than any others I had encountered.

I took a deep breath and charged at the bear with the torch as I had seen Mahtagwaysoo do when she first came with us. The bear decided that I was probably a good thing to stay away from and retreated out the cave entrance. Having two other torches backing me up, I was emboldened. This time, there were no cubs, and that made the bear a bit less dangerous.

We walked to the tunnel's mouth and looked for the village below. There was nothing there.

"Where did it go?" asked Mahtagwaysoo.

"It's there," said Abby and sighed. "But not right at the moment."

"We need to try again?" I asked.

"Looks like it." Turning to Mahtagwaysoo, Abby explained we had to go back in the cavern and do the ritual again.

"Why, there is no Blackfeather here?" she asked. "This is good."

"No, not in this time stream," Abby said. "We're in the right place, but not the right time."

"Oh," said Little Rabbit, sounding disappointed. "But it's good that he's not here!"

"Right," Abby said, "but there's nothing else here either."

"I thought it was odd there were no cubs this time," I said.

"What do you mean?" Abby asked.

"We've always seen cubs, so not seeing them now is unusual. Now I know why we're not seeing cubs. Ready to head back?"

"Let's get this over with," Abby said. "The sooner we return her to her time, the better."

We returned to the cavern, Mahtagwaysoo hefting her torch in one hand and her tomahawk in the other as she led us back to the altar. We went through the ritual again, and when we looked outside, we could see the village. Was it the right time? We'd have to go down there and find out. We couldn't just leave Little Rabbit in any time stream we happened to land in and call it good, then run back home. If the time weren't exactly right, the family that had disappeared from Grandmother Molly's village might never reappear.

The next time we tried, we weren't challenged by a bear and saw no cubs. That was good. The village looked just the same as when we left, and this time we kept an eye out for Blackfeather. The sun was setting, and the flames of a bonfire were reaching into the sky over the courtyard, red sparks disappearing into the increasing darkness. After we put out our torches and hid them just inside the tunnel's entrance, we started down the path to the main gate, darting behind trees so we wouldn't be easily seen. We moved one at a time, tree by tree, getting very close to the village gate.

There he was, standing by the opening of the stockade, backlit by the orange flames from the ceremonial fire pit. He looked like he had lost a fight with an angry bear. The arm that Mahtagwaysoo had pummeled with her tomahawk was wrapped with deerskin in what seemed to be a splint, and he limped a little, too. He wasn't smiling.

"There he is, that miserable...I...I just get so angry when I see him," Mahtagwaysoo sputtered as her face reddened and her knuckles grew white around the tomahawk's shaft.

"He'll get what he deserves," Abby said. Turning to me she asked, "Do you think we're in the right timeline now?"

"I get so lost in thinking about that," I sighed. "Let's be looking for differences just in case we're not, but so far everything looks okay. I sure don't want to be swimming in a time stream we don't belong in."

"That's okay, Charlie, I'll throw you a life ring if you go under," Abby said, and smiled.

Blackfeather moved his head slowly from side as if looking for something beyond the light of torches that burned at each side of the stockade's entrance. Several other young men were behind him. He didn't stay at the entrance for long. After a few minutes, he turned and walked away. Then we could see why. Gray Wolf came out from the shadows. He had a larger group of men with him. It was a safer time to show our faces. We came out from behind the giant trees and made our way to the opening of the stockade where Gray Wolf was standing. The men behind him were a reassuring sight.

Gray Wolf smiled as he saw us approach.

"It is good to see you again, Morning Star and Charlie Bear Claw," he greeted us. "But I'm not surprised to see you so soon. I imagine you had problems with Mahtagwaysoo coming along?"

"An entire family had disappeared," Abby explained.

"It is much better here," Little Rabbit said, seemingly relieved, "and the air smells much better."

"You're not worried about Blackfeather?" Gray Wolf asked.

"No!" she exclaimed, waving her tomahawk in the air. "I'll give him what he deserves if I can get close enough."

Gray Wolf looked at me. "Blackfeather has challenged you over Mahtagwaysoo."

"He's doing what?" Little Rabbit shouted. Her face was red with anger.

I looked at Abby, then back to Gray Wolf. "What does that mean?" I asked.

"There is an ancient tradition for settling disagreements," Gray Wolf said. "Blackfeather claims you took Mahtagwaysoo away from him, and he wants what he thinks is justice. He wants to have her back, and for you to be punished."

"I'm not his to have!" roared a defiant Mahtagwaysoo, shaking her tomahawk again. Abby placed her hand on Little Rabbit's shoulder to let her know she had support.

"That's crazy," Abby broke in. "Charlie doesn't want Mahtagwaysoo the way Blackfeather does."

"Maybe so," Gray Wolf said, "but he does have the right to challenge Charlie Bear Claw."

"How does he challenge me?" I asked.

"It will be after the potlatch tonight. Blackfeather will challenge you to fight him, and he'll do it publicly," Gray Wolf answered. "Each fighter may have two weapons, the staff and one other. The one who is left standing wins the respect and support of our tribe. If you lose, the tribe would see you as the Nodumkanwet. Everyone hates the Nodumkanwet."

"So, Charlie can just leave now?" Abby asked him.

"He may," Gray Wolf answered. He turned and looked at me. "If you leave, Blackfeather will be the winner by default. He will be the brave who defeated the Nodumkanwet." Parents would tell their children about the Nodumkanwet. It was like the Boogeyman. The kids were warned not to get close to the quagmire where it lived mostly to keep them away from the quicksand pits.

"And the tribe will support him?" Abby asked.

"It is our custom, and Mahtagwaysoo will be forced then to be his bride," Gray Wolf explained.

"I'm not doing anything like that," Mahtagwaysoo vowed. "That might be the custom, but I'll get out of here and find another clan before I get anywhere near that piece of moose turd."

This was one opportunity for some peace in her life that now depended on me. She could return with us, but Awasosqua thought it unwise; such a move could upset future events. It didn't appear that I had much of a choice about Blackfeather's challenge. I doubted I could win; I knew I had to try.

"Remember Hiram's story about making the right decision?" Abby asked.

"I do," I replied. "He told me to make the choice before it was made for me."

"Blackfeather has a weakness," Gray Wolf said. "He will do anything to possess a bride."

"He won't possess me!" Little Rabbit avowed. "And I won't bait in the trap!"

"You are what Blackfeather wants," Gray Wolf said to her.

"He won't get what he wants!" she nearly shouted.

"No, he won't," I promised. I reached into my pack basket. "Can someone put a long lanyard on this?" I handed Gray Wolf a baseball-sized rock. I asked for a counterweight to be tied to the opposite end of the lanyard. Gray Wolf passed the rock to Moosis with the instructions. The boy nodded his head, put it in his belt and ran off on his errand.

Gray Wolf explained what would happen. Blackfeather and I

would meet before the fire pit where we would each be given a staff about five feet long. We would face off, and the winner would have Mahtagwaysoo for his wife.

I looked at Abby when Gray Wolf finished explaining what could happen. She didn't look too happy, a huge frown telling me something was wrong.

"I only want her to have her freedom," I explained. "You have to know that, right?"

A little sheepish about her outburst, Abby's face reddened.

"If I win," I said, putting my hand on her shoulder, "she will be free to live her life without fear of Blackfeather. If I win, Gray Wolf will have no one to challenge his leadership."

"Are you any good with the staff?" Abby asked.

"Maybe," I replied. I hadn't talked much of my brothers teaching me how to use the staff. Besides, I didn't like to brag. The universe doesn't like it much hearing me boasting about anything. When I do, then things do not go well as a rule, so I keep some things unsaid.

We walked to the center of the courtyard where long tables were set out. I'd never imagined there would be so much food, and such a variety, too. There were large bowls that contained much of the same things we'd find at one of our own large celebratory gatherings in the village. There was corn, beans, potatoes just baked in the coals. Even though this was still May, the tribe had stored food from the year before in their root cellars and large baskets. Some were removing the spits from the fire and bringing them to another table where the meat was carved up. I never thought a knife knapped from stone would do as good a job as a steel one.

Members of the clan were gathering around the banquet tables, and soon we were helping ourselves to a delicious feast. Nolka and Moosis were right ahead of us as we sampled from all the dishes. There were plates, too. These were made from local clays and fired in a primitive kiln. There were large spoon like utensils for each serving dish. When Abby and I served ourselves, I couldn't help but wonder whether or not we were bringing in some deadly virus to a susceptible group.

I looked around for Blackfeather, but he didn't show up at the feast. When we finished eating, I saw Moosis leave the courtyard. Soon, he returned with something in his hand.

"Here comes Moosis," Abby said. Moosis ran up to us and handed me a pouch. After I secured it through my belt and nodded thanks, Moosis smiled and stepped back to the shadows.

The snake dance began, and we all took part in a long line around the blazing fire. The line dipped and wound about, here and there in the courtyard. The whole village seemed to be a part of the snake line that the villagers believed to be a challenge to the Nodumkanwet. Hopefully, it wouldn't show up! There was no sign of Blackfeather either.

Gray Wolf left for a few minutes and returned with a painted face and his ceremonial garb. He began the ceremony by saluting the spirits with a bowl of smoking sweet grass, pushing the offering to the four corners of the compass with a large eagle feather. This offering was nearly identical to the ceremony at the Nicatou settlement when I was given my name, *Charlie Bear Claw*. The practice seemed to have a soothing effect on my nerves. Some traditions don't seem to change. I was calmer and better focused on what may be ahead. Gray Wolf turned to the spectators who now formed a half moon around the fire, the orange light dancing on their faces, reminding the anxious audience the purpose of our battle and what the outcome would signify. He returned to the edge of the crowd to stand with Nolka and Mahtagwaysoo. Little Rabbit still held her tomahawk tightly in her hand.

One of the tribe approached me and with stretched out arms, handed me a stout and smooth shaft. He nodded, backed away, and disappeared into the shadows with the others.

I stood still, the staff in my hand, waiting for the event to begin. I worried if I would be successful in defeating Blackfeather. What if I killed him? How would that change the future? I had to defend myself, didn't I? Maybe we should have just dropped off Mahtagwaysoo and headed home instead. That would have been so much easier.

"Be careful, Charlie," Abby pleaded. "It's okay if you walk away, and we go home." She had read my mind.

"That wouldn't be okay for her, though," I said, pointing to Mahtagwaysoo, standing with Nolka, Moosis and Gray Wolf. "Even though she can handle him herself, I am the one who has to do this according to their customs."

We didn't have to wait long for Blackfeather to show up. The wind rose from the north, creating a small whirlwind by the fire, drawing up some sparks and coals from the edge. Like fireflies, the red coals outlined the funnel. Slowly, a tall figure appeared within and Blackfeather suddenly stood in front of us, a little smoke wafting from his shoulders. It was if he walked out of the flames themselves. The staff he held seemed larger than mine. This wasn't shaping up as an even match.

Blackfeather waited for me by the fire. I walked closer. The snake dance ended, and the drumming stopped. The crescent shaped group of observers went silent. The dancers mingled back with the rest of the tribe. Blackfeather was smiling, twirling his baton around his fingers, holding it mid staff and banging it into the ground several times, trying his best to intimidate me. It was working. I saw no need to waste my energy in showing my skills with the staff; I needed to focus on what would be coming at me.

He kicked the bottom of the staff into the air, grabbing it with his left hand while holding the other end in his right hand. With a scream, Blackfeather jumped forward and swung his staff high over his head with both hands, coming down at me. I was ready for his high hit and raised my staff in front of me with both hands to block his first strike, which glanced off to the side.

Blackfeather repositioned his hands and swung down low at my mid-section. I blocked that move as well. He leveraged his staff once more and we hit together, high above my shoulder. He seemed much stronger than I was, forcing my staff's end to the ground at my left. In an instant, Blackfeather had raised his staff and swung at my head. I expected the move. My brothers had taught me to watch for this, and I instinctively ducked low as his staff sailed harmlessly over my head.

I recognized his move as probably part of a sequence. I thought the next move was going to be a low swing at my legs, and I was right, jumping up as the staff passed under my feet. Part of Blackfeather's next move was to spin to his right, bringing his staff across my hip as he knocked mine free from one hand. White-hot pain sent me to the ground in a heap. The crowd groaned. I think I groaned, too, but I got right back up. Raising his staff again, he brought it down toward me, but I was expecting that. I stepped to the side while landing a blow on the back of his shoulder when he passed by. The crowd cheered.

I spun around and swung again, this time catching him on the center of his back, sending him to the ground once more. The crowd cheered again.

"Good hit, Charlie," I could hear Abby cry out. "Give him another one!"

Blackfeather got up with a sneer and angrily brushed the dirt from his leggings. I don't think he was expecting his opponent to be skilled enough to knock him down. He seemed to be thinking about his next move. I had to be careful. His anger was really what was driving him now, and that can seemingly double anyone's strength. It helped that my older brothers, Will and Sam, taught me this style of fighting. They had learned in some special army school before heading for the trenches and dying in France. And it wasn't the only thing they taught me about fighting.

I knew I had to stay focused, or things wouldn't end well. My hip really hurt. Blackfeather ran at me, holding his staff above his head, planning to pound me into the ground. I spun to the side the moment he was about to make contact, holding out my staff. He tripped over it, screeching like a hawk and collapsing in a cloud of dust. The crowd cheered again.

"Alright, Charlie!" Mahtagwaysoo exclaimed. "Do that again!" But I couldn't do the trick a second time. Blackfeather was wise to it now.

Again, Blackfeather dusted himself off. I think I'd rather face an angry nest of white tailed wasps. Again, he came at me, snarling and swinging his staff in a circle above his head. It was a good thing that I started to step away from him. Part way through the arc, he pointed the stick at me and lunged at the same time. When he did, he let out a spine tingling hawk-like shriek. It happened so fast. His staff caught me in the chest, sending me sprawling and out of breath. The crowd moaned. I thought I could hear a 'boo.'

"Come on, Charlie, get up!" Abby shouted.

Blackfeather waited for me to stand. He could have come right at me again, but he didn't. I had the impression he was a black panther playing with her food just before lunch. He wanted to hurt me a lot more, one blow at a time, I sensed. I stood up, brushed off my leggings. I raised my staff in both hands to my waist and crouched. *He won't get another chance*, I thought. I was getting angry. The south wind began to strengthen. The north wind was increasing at the same time, dust devils kicking up sand at the edge of the clearing.

We came at each other again, raising our staffs in attack and defense through the dust several times. I was getting tired; Blackfeather was not. I sensed some super strength coming from him, a strength that could easily overpower me, but I had some tricks of my own. I decided to change the game and thought the crowd, mostly my supporters, would accept it. Maybe he'd cry 'foul,' but I didn't care. He had to be defeated. I held my staff with my left hand while with my right hand I pulled out the bolo Moosis made for me. A bolt of lightning struck a tall pine on the edge of the clearing, the crack of thunder at the same time, the wind now beginning to howl. He was coming at me again but instead of a staff, he was holding a spear. I swung the lanyard about my head a few times and let the bolo fly towards him just like my brothers showed me. Swinging through the air, the long lanyard wrapped itself around Blackfeather's neck several times, choking him before he could react. Dropping the spear, he reached for his throat, trying to loosen the stricture. Before he could, I drove my staff into his center, doubling him in two, and finally, with a spin, I brought my staff down on the back of his head with a loud crack. Blackfeather went down in a heap. The winds subsided. The crowd cheered.

"Alright, Charlie!" Abby shouted.

"You got him good," cheered Mahtagwaysoo. I learned a lot from watching the mock battles the last time we were here. It's not a good idea to turn your back on your enemy. I walked up to the crumpled mess of Blackfeather, keeping away from his legs, my staff pointing towards his head. If he came to, I wanted him to see what could be coming his way should he come at me. Reaching down, I unwrapped the bolo from his neck. The raptor talon necklace came off with it. I held both up for everyone to see. The crowd roared.

Abby came to me, took the necklace from my hand and tied it around my neck. The crowd cheered again, and again. I really felt like Charlie Bear Claw for the first time. Blackfeather stayed down. I had knocked him out, but he wasn't dead. I thought I could see his chest move. I still didn't turn my back on his still form.

"Mahtagwaysoo is yours now, Charlie Bear Claw," Gray Wolf said, smiling at me as they walked toward me.

"I give her the freedom to choose another," I said. The crowd cheered and drumming began. Mahtagwaysoo ran to me, and with a big hug thanked me for saving her from Blackfeather although I think she could have done just as well. I hadn't noticed that Blackfeather was beginning to stir.

"Charlie, you can let go now," Abby said with a grin as she approached us. Mahtagwaysoo smiled too and stepped aside, Abby wrapping her arms around me. I could still see Blackfeather trying to get up.

"I think it's time for a celebration," Gray Wolf said. "Let us pass the pipe!" The ceremonial pipe was brought out. It was almost as long as the staffs! Moosis and his friends were playing with sticks, pretending to act out the fight they had just seen to the howls of the grownups. I was seeing the next generation of braves in training.

"I don't think I want to go home, Abby," I said. She smiled at me; I smiled back. "We have friends here now. This is such a warm, welcoming family."

"I know, Charlie," Abby said. "Part of me wants to stay, too, but you know we don't belong here. It's not our time, is it?"

"You're right," I practically whispered.

"Sorry, can't quite hear you," Abby complained.

"You're right," I said again, a little louder, and laughed. Another crack of lightning and boom of thunder surprised us all.

"Look!" someone shouted. We turned. There beside the fire was Blackfeather, standing with his arms folded, defiantly, across his chest. His eyes seemed to glow red. Then he seemed to fade away. I could see the fire through him. The north wind rose again, leaves blew about and sparks flew as what had been Blackfeather was now Ki'kwa'jenu, hovering in the air taller than a totem pole.

"Blackfeather is Ki'kwa'jenu," someone shouted from the crowd. Villagers ran in every direction, deciding to keep watch from the safety of the trees that ringed the courtyard.

Ki'kwa'jenu's black wings were raising dust, his claws, red-tipped with what looked like blood, reaching for the ground as he landed. Hiram was right about the Nighthawk's size. I looked at its eyes, glowing red coals, burning through me. I had to look away. He wasn't getting into my head! Ki'kwa'jenu's power was much stronger in this time, and this Nighthawk could be seen by everyone, not just me as a result. This wasn't Blackfeather in a costume. Blackfeather was the human form Ki'kwa'jenu had taken. Now I understood how he was so good at locating game. I guess I wasn't that surprised. Almost anything could happen in this time stream.

"What does it want?" I heard murmuring from the crowd.

"I don't think it's a what. It's a 'who,'" I said. "He wants me." I stepped toward the figure at the edge of the firelight as I grabbed the staff from the ground.

"No, Charlie," Abby cried out. "Don't go that close, please, Charlie," she begged.

"I have to face him," I said. "The dreams have to stop," letting Abby's hand drop away from my arm. I moved closer.

She turned to Gray Wolf. "Can't you talk some sense into him?" Abby asked. "He has to decide for himself," Gray Wolf said. I turned and walked toward Ki'kwa'jenu. The spirit's eyes were coal red, and I could see the sharpness of its beak. One chomp, I thought, and this

Nighthawk could cut a moose in half. Its fishy breath was enough to suffocate someone.

Nolka had her arms around Abby. Mahtagwaysoo stood near them shaking her tomahawk and yelling, her face red in anger, her body seemed tensely coiled, ready to spring like a cobra at its prey. I could see tears glistening on Abby's cheek. Gray Wolf held a white-knuckled grip on the ceremonial pipe.

"There is only one person I want," Ki'kwa'jenu said in a raspy voice, barely above a whisper as his bright red eyes drilled into me, but then the Nighthawk turned in another direction. Flapping its wings, the dust rose and sparks blew from the bonfire. The villagers stayed in the shadows fearing for their lives. Mahtagwaysoo was waving her tomahawk. The Nighthawk did not want me. Ki'kwa'jenu reached out and grabbed Mahtagwaysoo with his bloody red talons. In an instant, the raptor dissolved into the darkness with his prey screaming curses. Little Rabbit's tomahawk was on the ground where she had dropped it as she was lifted into the air. Ki'kwa'jenu flew away, Mahtagwaysoo held fast, screaming curses and flailing her arms and legs. The screams from the onlookers drowned out the sounds from the black wings as it disappeared. Nolka was sobbing on her father's shoulder, and Moosis' little sister clung to her mother's leg in fear.

Abby came over to me, her hand on my shoulder. "Charlie?" she said. "You okay?" And with that, Ki'kwa'jenu's spell was broken. I hoped I would never see his black wings again, either following us or in my dreams.

"He could have taken you, Charlie!" Abby said, hugging me tight. "Poor Mahtagwaysoo, she didn't have a chance."

"He took someone he could more easily prey on," I explained. "But that's not why he's been following me, been in my dreams so much," I said.

"Why?" asked Abby. I looked at Gray Wolf who smiled.

"Because Ki'kwa'jenu wants your power of Sowanakik," Gray Wolf said. "It was all about the south wind. You haven't heard all the stories, Charlie. It is believed that Ki'kwa'jenu has sought the power of all the spirit winds."

"But he took Mahtagwaysoo and not me. Why?" I asked.

"Maybe the Nighthawk wants you to pay him a visit," Gray Wolf suggested. "He might still have plans for you in time."

That time thing again….which time? Here and now or after we get back home? And did Ki'kwa'jenu want me to rescue her? Was the

Nighthawk luring me to his aerie?

"How do we get Mahtagwaysoo back?" I asked. "She must be terrified."

"The Nighthawk will take her to his nest," Gray Wolf said. "Soon, she will meet her fate, but there might be time to rescue her."

"If we could find his nest, do you think we could free her?" I asked Gray Wolf. I wondered if this was some sort of Nighthawk plan. Lure me to its nest, then take my power.

"It's possible," Gray Wolf explained. " But you must guard your own power. You must find the shaman who knows the location of Ki'kwa'jenu's nest."

"Where do we find him?" I asked.

"He lives near the Gathering Place at the head of Schunk'awke where, our stories tell us, you can find the nest," Gray Wolf said. "He once told me that he knows where it is. His name is Moskwaso."

Ki'kwa'jenu
(The Nighthawk)
Chapter 17

We packed dried venison and smoked salmon, a little corn meal and some acorn flour. At least we'd eat well. Young Moosis led us to a row of canoes upside down and draped over two logs to keep them off the ground. I'd never seen such birch bark canoes before. They looked rugged enough for rapids. The bark was thick, sewn and tarred together with pine pitch. The gunnels that ran from end to end were stout pieces of ash sapling, split down the middle. Thwarts were ash, too. It was easy enough to split apart by pounding. Two men were doing that as we waited for Gray Wolf. Soon, he arrived.

"You will need a guide," Gray Wolf said. "Moosis will be going with you. He's light, doesn't eat much and knows the way."

Moosis was sharp and quick, a few years younger than me. Gray Wolf helped us select the best canoe.

"That one has good eyes," he said, pointing to large painted eyes on each side of the bow.

"Why eyes?" I asked Abby.

"It's so the canoe can see the rocks," she explained. "It's the paddler's good luck charm."

We were given three paddles and a fourth for a spare. Gray Wolf handed Moosis a map he had drawn on birch bark with a piece of

141

charcoal. After we loaded our packs, we got in and began the trip down the stream to the river that flowed from *Schunk'awke*, an old name for Chesuncook Lake. This time we were going against the current. We poled along the edge of the big river, out of the main flow, "the place of descending rocks," keeping in the eddies on what we called the Penobscot River.

When we got to Nesourdnahunk Stream, we began our first carry over a large beaver dam at the stream's opening into the river. The carries were easier because Moosis was helping. We paddled for more than a mile until we came to another beaver dam and repeated the process, unload, carry over the beaver dam, re-load and continue paddling. Like steps of water, we climbed up the stream to Mud Pond. Once there, we began the descent down Mud Pond Stream, over five more beaver dams, and finally to the shore of Schunk'awke.

"I don't remember so many beaver dams on this stream," I said.

"Maybe it's because the Voyagers trapped them all out?" Abby suggested. "Without the beavers, there'd be no steps." I remembered seeing this streambed as it entered the lake when Father took me over to Red Brook. Mud Pond Stream was a rock garden with barely a trickle of water snaking through the exposed boulders. Abby was right.

The lake was too rough to paddle. We waited near the shore until evening when the roaring wind that tore the foam off the tops of the whitecaps coming down the lake might die down. Although our birch bark canoe could withstand big waves like the ones we were watching wash violently by, paddling into the wind would be useless even with three of us. We had to wait on shore until the wind dropped.

"Remember the reason Mahtagwaysoo had to come back?" I asked Abby while Moosis was trying his hand at catching dinner.

"The Mitchell family that disappeared?" she clarified.

"That's the thing," I said. "Mahtagwaysoo may be lost to us, but somehow she has to survive or that family won't exist in our time."

"So you're saying it's a given that we'll get her back?" Abby asked.

"No, but the consequences of us not succeeding are not so good for that family," I said.

By early evening the wind had calmed, and the sky cleared. The stars seemed so close. On nights like this, the earth cooled faster than on cloudy nights, and we might even see a frost. It was still early spring. When the lake had more ripples than whitecaps, and the big swells disappeared, we launched the canoe and paddled north to the

Gathering Place. It was now an entire day since Ki'kwa'jenu had taken Mahtagwaysoo. I wished we could make better time.

"I didn't know the lake was named for Canada geese," I said.

"I'm not surprised," came Abby's response. "My dad and I used to see hundreds at a time lift off from Brandy Pond on the way upriver to Second Falls."

"I get the sense that there are more than hundreds in this time," I offered.

"I think so, too. Probably thousands. Look at the size of the fish they catch here; we have minnows by comparison."

"It's the dams and running wood down the rivers," I said, "that's driven the numbers way down."

"Look at the fires ahead," Moosis pointed out. I looked far ahead and could see three bright fires on the distant shore. These were signal fires to guide canoes to the annual potlatch at the Gathering Place. We could see another canoe ahead of us. It had probably come down a different stream, but the destination was the same.

The lake we knew so well was very different now, narrow almost like a river with wide expanses of marsh grass along each side. The features of the shoreline that I knew didn't exist now. I would have to imagine what the shore would look like under another twenty-five feet of water above us. Here and there, we saw a sandy beach where one could set up camp if the wind rose suddenly. The lake's surface had calmed even more, and now we could see the reflection of the three signal fires on the surface of nearly mirror calm water.

"See the long houses?" Abby asked. "I didn't think there would be so many." Long houses dotted the flats beyond the sandy beach and the marsh grass. When we got closer to the beach and signal fires, we could make out racks of drying fish and a game pole with moose and deer hanging from it.

"They come back every year," Abby said from the stern. I still wasn't allowed to steer. "They come from the coast for the fish and the berries. When family groups intermarry, this annual gathering might be the only time to see your own family since the year before."

"I have many cousins here," Moosis added, "but I see them maybe once or twice a year when we go to the coast. That's when the snow comes."

We paddled towards the firelight. The shore was of fine, nearly white sand. When we got closer, I could see people standing around the fires. The bow of the canoe came within a few feet of the sandy shore when Moosis stepped out into the water to keep the canoe from hitting the shore. Birch bark was strong, but the paddler still had to be careful of rocks and sand that could wear it down and cause problems later. He steadied the canoe while I got out. Then it was my turn to hold it while Abby uncoiled her long legs, stepped out and stood in the shallow water beside the stern. We picked the canoe up and turned it upside down, resting it on two small logs nearby and placing the paddles underneath. Our packs were on the shore.

Fireflies and moths were hovering near the signal fire. Bats swooped down from the darkness and flew away with their meal. We could hear the *crunch* of a crushed moth as the bat's jaws closed on its catch.

"What tribe are you from?" The voice seemed to come from the flames, but it was a young girl standing in front of the fire, back lit with orange light.

"Nicatou," Abby said. "We've come to see Moskwaso."

"Gray Wolf sent you?" she asked.

"Yes," Abby replied.

"Who is your family?" she asked. Abby thought a moment. I could see her working out a reply.

"Awasosqua," Abby said. "I'm a cousin."

"I can take you to his lodge," she said, satisfied that we were no threat. "But first you should pay your respects to our leader, Old Bezo. We grabbed our packs and followed.

"I'm going to see my cousins," Moosis said. "I'll meet you here in an hour, okay?" and he ran toward the row of long houses before we could even acknowledge him.

"Bobcat," Abby whispered to me before I could ask what 'Bezo' meant. "I think he's their chief." The girl led us to a small, domed hut. Crisscrossed with alder poles, it had a doorway like the ones in the old village. She pulled away the hide covering the door and disappeared inside, the hide flapping back into place. In a moment she returned and beckoned us inside. We were introduced to Old Bezo, sitting on some furs and leaning against a fur-draped log the hut seemed to have been built around. He looked pretty wiry for an older chieftain.

"You've come a long way from Nicatou. How is Gray Wolf?" he asked.

"He's well," Abby said. Old Bezo was looking us over. "We ask permission to see Moskwaso."

"Why do you want to see our shaman?" he asked.

"One of our people was taken by the Nighthawk," Abby explained. "Gray Wolf sent us here to find your shaman, Moskwaso. We think he can help us get her back."

"If you anger the Nighthawk, our village could be in danger. We have an uneasy peace with it now and have not lost anyone for a long time. It is not a good idea to go to the nest in the cliff." As the old man stood, we could hear his bones creak. "But, if I allow you to go, you must promise to bring back a feather for everyone in the tribe. Then, if the Nighthawk is angry with your visit, our people can be protected."

"Feathers?" Abby asked. "We can do that." I looked at her wondering how that was going to happen.

"Gray Wolf is a good friend. Moskwaso lives just down the path," Old Bezo replied.

"At least we don't have to hunt all over for Moskwaso. We wouldn't have had time for that," I said after we thanked Old Bezo and were walking out of the hut. Abby nodded in agreement. Our guide was waiting for us and took us to the doorway several longhouses down the path. A woman had just stepped from the doorway as we approached. I think word spread pretty fast in the village. I looked around for Moosis but didn't see him.

"They are here to see Moskwaso," our guide explained to her, and having delivered her charges safely, turned and walked away in the direction we had come. The woman rapped on the pole that formed part of the doorway and pulled aside the deerskin tarp that covered the opening, motioning us to enter.

"This place is really big," I said as soon as I went through the low doorway.

"I know. It looks like several families are living here now," Abby replied.

Moskwaso's long house had three distinct cooking fires, holes in the roof above each one, a few partitions for privacy in the sleeping areas. Everything else was open. Some were walking through the family areas. Children played everywhere except the little alcove where Moskwaso sat on a woven blanket. A few torches along the walls gave out plenty of light. What caught my eye was a small stone with three depressions containing some kind of clear oil on which three yellow flames danced. What kind of oil? I wondered. Did it come with them from the coast, their winter residence? The brightly colored woven blanket Moskwaso sat on wasn't something I had seen before in Gray Wolf's village. My guess was the blanket came from the same place the oil lamp came from, some trading center near their winter home. Moskwaso wore a headband with several symbols woven around it. Bands of wampum were around his neck and each wrist was circled with narrow bands of green and red shells. On the wall behind him were talons and large black feathers that looked as if they had come from a Nighthawk.

"You come from Nicatou?" Moskwaso asked, looking us over.

"Welcome from Gray Wolf," Abby said. Moskwaso drew on his pipe and then looked at her. "Young Moosis has guided us here tonight."

"Gray Wolf is a good ally," he said, "and you couldn't have a better guide than young Moosis." He smiled at the thought. "He's a distant nephew."

"We have lost someone to the Nighthawk," she explained, not wanting to get into family relationships. "Gray Wolf sent us to find you in hopes of learning where its nest is."

"Ki'kwa'jenu will be a difficult adversary," he said. "If I tell you where the nest is, what will you do?"

"We'll go there and rescue the woman he took from our tribe," Abby said. Moskwaso raised one eyebrow.

"You make it sound easy," he observed. "Do you really think you can just walk in there, find your friend or more likely what's left of her, and come back?" He looked at my necklaces of bear claws and Nighthawk talons. "Although I imagine you had more skill than luck to get that necklace from Blackfeather."

"You know who he really is? I asked.

"There are many stories about the Nighthawk changing to a human form, so yes, we all know who he is," Moskwaso said. "The Nighthawk morphed into a young maiden just to trap the spirit of my grandfather."

"Was your grandfather okay?" Abby asked.

"He could tell she wasn't what she appeared to be, and he was able to get away." Moskwaso added something to a pipe he had been holding in his hand.

I shouldn't have been surprised that he knew about Blackfeather. News travels between villages almost as fast as it does within one. I wanted to tell him about Blackfeather morphing into the Nighthawk or the other way around, but that would have taken too long. I'm not sure I understood it myself.

"We really need your help," I pleaded. "The longer we delay, the less likely she will survive." Moskwaso thought a moment. Then, he nodded.

"Moosis can lead you," he said. "I will show him the path."

"Thank you, Moskwaso," Abby said. "We'll send in Moosis as soon as we find him. He's visiting his cousins right now."

"There is one more thing," said Moskwaso. "Once you have entered the nest, a feather from the Nighthawk worn in the headband will protect you from being taken away yourselves. But be careful; the feather's power does not work well when you are close to the aerie."

"Old Bezo asked us to bring feathers back for your village. Now I understand why," I said. We thanked him again and went back to speak with Old Bezo before leaving the village.

"We will be traveling to the nest of the Nighthawk," Abby told him. "Moskwaso will show Moosis the path."

"And if you do not return?" Old Bezo asked.

"We'll be back," answered Abby firmly. "And there will be someone else with us when we do. Please keep an eye on our canoe. It belongs to Gray Wolf." Old Bezo nodded his head and raised his hand in good-bye. We walked outside. Out from the shadows, Moosis came running down the path to us.

"Did you see your cousins?" Abby asked.

Catching his breath, Moosis said, "I did. They wanted to come with us, but I said not to."

"Smart thing to stay here," I said. I was wishing at times I could join them in the comfort of their hut, but a life was at stake here. More than one if you counted descendants who would never be.

"You need to go to Moskwaso's hut now," I said. "He's going to draw you a map to the aerie." Moosis ran off to the hut and disappeared under its doorway flap. In a few minutes, he popped out and gestured for us to come with him. We were following a ten-year-old into the darkness where we could be picked apart by a giant hawk, limb by limb. I was more than a little anxious. It was going to be difficult not to bring up a good gust from Sowanakik the way I was feeling.

We were lucky to have a clear night. I don't remember seeing so many stars so close, and so bright. The air was pristine. There was no factory smoke to dim the view. I could see the Big Dipper right where it was supposed to be. That the handle seemed a little straighter was the only difference I could see in the sky. There was enough starlight so we didn't need torches that might announce our visit. Our path followed a stream's bank. When we came to a fallen tree, we were able to thread our way between the branches and got to the other side with dry feet. There was a small rise that led to a plateau. We could see the Nighthawk's nest tucked into an opening part way up a sheer cliff. There, we would find Mahtagwaysoo- I hoped in one piece. The light of the signal fires glistened off the water cascading down the sheer ledge like ribbons of molten silver.

"I see two ways to get there," I said, looking up at the cliff.

"Which are?" Abby asked while she translated for Moosis.

"Climb the cliff from below or drop down from above," I said.

"There is a third way," Moosis said.

"Which is?" I asked.

"There's a path that starts over there," Moosis pointed, "and winds up through the rock inside the cliff in that old fissure in front of us. According to Moskwaso, the tunnel comes out right at the back edge of the Nighthawk's nest."

"Has anyone ever done this?" I asked.

"And lived?" Abby added.

"Yeah, that too," I said. We never did get an answer.

"This is sacred ground," Moosis said. Our ancestors are there." Moosis pointed at the opening in the woods just before us. Just beyond it, we could see narrow platforms elevated on posts in between the wide spaced trees. These were not in neat rows like the headstones at Pleasant View Cemetery. These resting places were put wherever the ground would permit it.

"That's where your father is, isn't it?" Abby asked him.

"It is," he said in a whisper. "To show respect to the ancestors, we'll need to be quiet while we walk through," he whispered. "My father's spirit may not be at peace yet." Moosis' father had been buried there not long ago, Abby told me. There was a time period after death when the spirit apologized for any wrongs committed during life. Once making amends, the spirit was free to roam the heavens. We walked along the starlit path.

I could see the raised platforms in the sandy soil. Four upright poles wedged in between rocks stood six feet high, each ending in a 'Y.' Two poles, each eight feet long, rested there and supported a mat of smaller poles that made the platform on which the body was laid to rest. There were dozens of these mausoleums of the woods on the mesa just before the path that led to the cliffs where the Nighthawk lived. I had to wonder why this resting place was sited close to the Nighthawk's nest. Moosis stopped after the first few we passed. Tassels, spears, shields and beaded wampum decorated most. Then we saw what he was looking at.

"See that haze?" Abby whispered to me. A mist seemed to

appear, but then vanished.

"I just saw it fade away," I said. Moosis turned and motioned for us to follow him.

"What was that?" Abby asked.

"I don't think I want to know," I replied.

"Stay close behind me," Moosis warned. "Sometimes the spirits will reach out for you and will want you to stay." We closed ranks and followed Moosis, practically stepping on his heels. This didn't look like a place we'd like to stay in for long.

The bodies were wrapped in hides with the fur on the inside. Bands of sinew bound them at regular intervals. Totems hung from most of the poles, either dangling from the top or tied around a crosspiece. Dream catchers were everywhere. I didn't think to ask why spirits needed dream catchers; maybe they had dreams like the living. You could tell a resting place for a well-loved brave, like Moosis' father, just from the number of decorated shields on the posts that held the body in the air, far from the jaws of passing wolves. Adorned with tassels and interlaced with porcupine quills, each shield was a work of art in both form and function. His father's resting place was well cared for.

"Come on," Moosis said. "It's this way." We hurried after him, watching our step on the boulders the closer we got to the bottom of the cliff ahead of us. It wasn't easy keeping up with Moosis; he hopped from boulder to boulder like a rabbit.

"There's the crevasse," Abby said. She pointed to a cleft in the rock. "We can get the feathers first," Abby plotted. "And then we will be protected. Here, put on this headband." She handed me a headband, and she had one already for herself. "I have a spare in case Mahtagwaysoo needs one, and Moosis has his own." We put on the headbands. "Hey, yours is prettier than mine!"

"Funny. Let's get going before I decide I need to go home and wake up from this nightmare," I said. "I mean we're climbing a cliff in the middle of the night and......" Before I could sputter out the rest, Abby put her hand on my shoulder.

"Take a deep breath, Charlie. Relax. Just breathe. The south wind has really kicked up." And soon I calmed down. The rising winds around us calmed as well.

Moosis led us into the crevasse. When we pulled ourselves up on a large boulder, we were able to drop back down on the other side. From there the mountain goat path snaked about on an uphill climb, like S-turns around a mountain, but this time the road was inside. Abby had two stones that sparked when hit together, and she easily lit one of the two torches we had brought with us. I held the burning torch while Abby climbed ahead of me into the tunnel.

"I hope Ki'kwa'jenu doesn't see us coming," I said. Moosis tensed up at the mention of the Nighthawk's name.

"It's probably out doing Nighthawk stuff, getting more food for the babies," Abby replied. "It may wait a while before eating dinner. I hope."

"Babies?" I nearly shouted. "You mean there will be more of them in there?"

"This is going to be easier than you think it will be, Charlie. We have to be really quiet now. Any noise we make might telegraph right up this crevasse to the nest." That didn't make me feel any better.

We made our way through the crevasse deep in the hill. It was like being in a giant cave. We kept working our way towards a shelf that Moosis said was the back entrance to the aerie. I jammed the torch between two rocks and peered around a large rock that was partially blocking the tunnel just ahead. Any light now would make us an easy target. We could see right into the aerie and were safe as long as we stayed behind the boulder.

Moonlight streamed into the opening in front of us, a tall void in solid rock. The edge of the cliff was a straight line across the ledge at the cave's mouth. Large sticks formed a tall lip that made up the nest, taking up the entire area. There were a few bones around, human or not I couldn't tell and really didn't want to know. Two giant speckled eggs were in the center. Each one was over two feet high. One had begun to crack. Babies would soon be ready for their first meal. We didn't want to be on the menu.

"Did you hear that?" I asked.

"Hear what?" Abby said.

"Over there," I pointed. "I heard someone moan."

And there, stretched out along the far side of the nest, was Mahtagwaysoo. She was on Ki'kwa'jenu's menu for the new arrivals' first meal.

"What's the plan again?" Abby asked.

"Get the feathers and put them on, I said. "Let's start looking. Remember, we promised to collect them for the village."

In a few minutes all of us had the feathers in place, Abby had an extra one for Mahtagwaysoo and Abby's pack was stuffed full for the villagers. Moosis stayed behind the boulder, refusing to come into the nest area in case Ki'kwa'jenu came back earlier than expected. *Smart kid*, I thought.

"Okay," I said. "Let's go get her." We walked along the edge of the nest and came to Mahtagwaysoo's side.

Abby shook her shoulder. "Mahtagwaysoo," she whispered. "Wake up!" She groaned. "Charlie, hand me your water skin." I passed it to her. Abby opened it and began to splash a little water on Mahtagwaysoo's face who sputtered and started to sit up.

"Here," Abby said. "Drink." Mahtagwaysoo drank from the flask. "Here's some dried fish." Abby handed her a small strip of dried salmon.

"We need to get out of here," I urged. There was no sign of the Nighthawk.

"Here, put this feather in her headband," Abby said to me, and she handed me one of the feathers from her headband.

I followed orders, and soon Mahtagwaysoo was able to stand. The Nighthawk's claws hadn't hurt her. We walked around the side of the nest and were at the boulder at the start of the tunnel when we heard the flapping of wings. Ki'kwa'jenu had returned, and the Nighthawk was not happy. It perched on the very edge of the opening in the cliff and dropped the unlucky raccoon from its beak as its ear-piercing screeches filled the nest area.

"Abby, you lead her back to Moosis. I'm right behind. Hurry!" I shouted at her. They disappeared behind the boulder, leaving the torch so I could find my way to them. Louder shrieking from the angered spirit nearly ruptured my eardrums.

"Come on, Charlie!" Abby cried out from the safety of the other side of the boulder. "We've got to go now!"

I had my eye on a stick about five feet long and as thick as my thumb. It was right at my feet. *It's the perfect size*, I thought. I'd have one chance before he snapped the staff and then me in two pieces with his powerful beak. The feather I wore didn't seem to stop his advance. I was getting angrier by the moment, angry at the loss of Mother and Tommy, the fears, what the spirit tried to do to an innocent Mahtagwaysoo, and to others, too. The south wind began to rise, and after a few seconds of howling across the nest's opening in the cliff, the wind began to pour into the nest area.

"Now's your chance," I shouted at it. "Come and get me." I was ready with the staff when the giant raptor began to disappear behind a sudden misty cloud. As the wind dispersed the mist, there was

Blackfeather, standing taller than ever before. He reached down and grabbed a stick from the nest. It was too long to fight with, but he broke it to size over his knee and raised it to take a swing at me. I was ready for him, dodging the staff, then spinning around and striking hard on its side. Blackfeather came at me again, but this time I turned and ducked toward the cave's opening, spinning once more and hitting him behind the knees. He went down in a clump really close to the two eggs. I was still pretty steamed, and the south wind continued to rise. Blackfeather got up and came at me again, but this time his staff connected with my gut, knocking the wind out of me and my staff out of my hands. I was now on my back, my head nearly hanging over the cliff, my shoulders resting against two rocks. If those rocks had not been there, I would have been sucked out of the cave by the draft of the ever-increasing south wind. Blackfeather brought his staff over his head, intending to smash out my brains. Just as the staff began its downward arc, I sat up and grabbed it, pulling Blackfeather down toward me. At the same moment, the wind increased in intensity creating a draft that sucked Blackfeather out over the lip of the aerie. I turned just in time to see him morph again into Ki'kwa'jenu and soar away into the darkness. As I calmed, so did the wind, and I hurried back to the rear of the aerie, grabbed Abby's torch, and scampered around the boulder where Moosis, Abby and Mahtagwaysoo were waiting.

"Let's go!" I shouted. "We don't have much time before he comes after us." We climbed back down the fissure and stopped when we reached the outside mesa where Moosis doused the torch in a rivulet that wound through the larger rocks beside us, disappearing and then reappearing, making its way to the lake below. There was still plenty of starlight, and we had no difficulty making our way through a landscape of black and white, like an old photograph. We stopped for Mahtagwaysoo to rest.

"We shouldn't stop for long," I warned her. "It's still out there, and not too happy."

"She has to, Charlie, just a little. Remember, she hasn't eaten for two days," Abby said.

"Look out!" I shouted. Ki'kwa'jenu buzzed over our heads. It pulled away at the last minute. We ducked under the sharp talons, the giant bird grasping at the empty air where we had just stood.

"That was too close! I don't think these feathers are doing their job," said Abby, helping Mahtagwaysoo along. Abby held one arm and I held on to the other. We followed Moosis down the talus pile at the bottom of the crevasse. The Nighthawk was coming around for another run at us. Looking over my shoulder, I could see two bright red eyes closing in.

"Duck!" I shouted. We dropped down between the boulders, the air hissing in pulses from the black wings that buzzed over our heads.

"I thought these feathers were supposed to protect us!" Abby said.

"Maybe they are, and it's why we're not in pieces at the bottom of his nest!"

I could see coal-red eyes in the distance when Ki'kwa'jenu banked around for another attempt. We made it into the burial ground.

"These burial platforms will give us some cover," Abby said, as we ducked between two. Moosis didn't look happy to be cowering under one of his relatives. After every attempt failed, we scampered to the next platform. Soon, we'd be under the last one.

"But what happens when we get to the end?" I asked.

The Nighthawk came in from the side, skimming the tops of the platforms when the same white miasma we saw on the way to the nest re-appeared. This time the white mist took the shape of a brave dressed in leggings, protective bands of moose skin on his arms, holding a shield in one hand and a spear in the other.

"Go behind me," it said. "I will keep Ki'kwa'jenu busy."

Moosis was terrified seeing his father's form beside us. When I put my hand on his shoulder to urge him on, he turned and led us through the end of the burial ground. Loud screeching noises from behind propelled us forward. Moosis stayed in the lead. We found our way out of the forest faster than we did on the way in.

"I hope Ki'kwa'jenu doesn't bother the village here," I said. Abby asked Moosis about it.

"My father's spirit will protect it," he explained. As he spoke, Moosis held his head high and stood straight, proud of his father. Soon, we arrived back at the summer village at the Goose Place, the welcoming firelight racing down the path to meet us as we walked out of the darkness.

"Hey, Moosis!" we heard a young voice shout.

"It's my cousins," Moosis explained.

"See if you can find someone to help Mahtagwaysoo. She's pretty well banged up," I said. Moosis ran to his cousin, and they went for help.

Two women appeared and took Mahtagwaysoo into one of the

huts. There, they bathed and fed her, tended to her cuts and scrapes, while Abby and I got the canoe ready for a fourth. Moosis was still visiting his cousins. Old Bezo arranged for us to stay with a nearby family. We would leave the village in the morning. There were no black wings in my dreams that night.

Schunk'awke
(The Goose Place)
Chapter 18

We settled into the canoe at dawn, and with a light tail wind we began our trip back down the lake.

"Mt. Katahdin looks cold this morning," Abby said.

"I can see the snow," I said. "Seems there's always snow on the tableland up to the summit, except for maybe July." Mahtagwaysoo was quiet this morning. I can't imagine what she must have gone through in the Nighthawk's nest and how Moosis was able to pass by his father's spirit on our way out. Black wings flew high above us when we left shore, but there was no other sign of the Nighthawk after that. I hoped his black feathers in our headbands would ward him off now that we were far away from his nest and his source of strength.

"We won't have snow for a while yet," Moosis said. "First, the berries need to ripen and the salmon need to run. Then, we go back to the coast."

"How long does that trip take you?" I asked.

"Five days to Wiscasset," Moosis replied.

"I almost don't recognize this place," I said. Off to our right was what would become Graveyard Point. The distant ridgelines looked exactly the same, but the lakeshore was much different. Hundreds of feet of marsh grass pushed out from the forest to the lake's edge on both sides. In a few places the trees came right to the water, but not often. The slope was gradual. If the water went up a few inches from heavy rains, the grasslands would be under water. The only exception was a narrower section of marsh grass in front of what would become the Smith Farm on the north side of Gero. There, the glacial river had pushed away the soil from the ledge, gave up on eroding the shoreline, and took a sharp turn down the lake to Ripogenus Gorge, 'the place of rainbows.'

"Let's get to shore and take a closer look at where we'll be living someday," I said.

"We can follow that brook to shore," Abby pointed out. We landed the canoe at what I thought would later be Canoe Brook. Moosis stayed with Mahtagwaysoo. Abby and I walked along the edge of the marsh grass by the tree line to the point.

"That's where the Inn will be." I pointed out the location to Abby.

"I can almost see the fields and barns," she said. We walked to the level area where the cemetery would be before the water level raised by the dams at Chesuncook and later Ripogenus. I began to pace off thirty steps to the west.

"What are you doing?" Abby asked.

"Making an estimate of how far from that boulder I'm standing," I said.

"Okay, so what's going on?" Abby asked again.

"Moskwaso gave me this nice spear point just before we left," I explained. "And I'm going to bury it here. For now." I showed Abby a six-inch spear point made from Munsungan Chert, so thin it was translucent, serrations along both sides and sharp like a razor.

"I guess, Charlie, but you're a real mystery sometimes. Why bury it?"

"When we get back, I want to be able to find it. Wouldn't it be neat to touch something in our time that came from Moosis?" I told her, covering it over with sod. "Time to go." We walked along the shore back to the canoe. We paddled around the point and into a tail wind. Mahtagwaysoo began fussing with a thin deer hide and a paddle. Abby asked her what she was doing, and soon a small deerskin sail supported by paddles was pushing us down the lake. All Abby had to do was steer.

"How's Mahtagwaysoo doing?" I asked. "She seems to have calmed down since last night." Abby and Mahtagwaysoo had talked a bit.

"She's okay, Charlie, still a little rattled. She keeps looking over her shoulder, doesn't she?" Abby pointed out. With a nice tail wind and the sail doing the work of many paddlers, we were making much better time down the lake than when we came up.

We sailed the canoe down the lake for an hour. When we got close to Mud Pond Stream, we took down the sail and paddled to shore. Mahtagwaysoo seemed tired from her ordeal; we decided to have something to eat and rest before moving on.

"How are you doing?" I asked Little Rabbit. She looked exhausted, even her hair looked tired.

"Okay," she replied. "I keep seeing the bones woven into the nest whenever I close my eyes." She stared off to the woods. A moment passed. "I fought those talons, but Ki'kwa'jenu wouldn't let me go."

"I can only imagine," I said. "But the beast could have dropped you if you had succeeded."

"I thought of that and decided to wait until we landed. But by that time, I had passed out."

"I'm not surprised," I said. "The Nighthawk can be pretty scary." We got our gear together for the first carry up the stream.

The first beaver dam was a hundred feet in, safe from the crashing waves off the lake. Once we carried over it, we began the first of many liquid steps to the headwaters of Nesourdnahunk Stream. We carried over more beaver dams and through the woods. After reaching the river below Nesourdnahunk Falls, we had just a few more rapids to carry around. Soon, we were at Gray Wolf's village.

Word spread through the tribe like a wildfire, and in moments nearly everyone had gathered around Gray Wolf to greet Mahtagwaysoo's safe return. Nolka ran to embrace her and Moosis. I hadn't seen her smile since the night I defeated Blackfeather. Mahtagwaysoo smiled as her friends embraced her.

We gathered around the bonfire later that evening and had a great feast. The snake dance seemed to go on forever. Finally, the drumming quieted, and we turned in for the night in one of Gray Wolf's lodges.

We had seen no more signs of the black wings since the time in the canoe when he must have seen all three of his feathers and veered away.

"You have done well, Charlie Bear Claw, and you too, Abby, granddaughter of my Awasosqua. We are glad to have Mahtagwaysoo with us again," Gray Wolf said.

The next morning, we said our good-byes to everyone. Moosis

stood beside his grandfather; Gray Wolf saluted us. Some followed us to the opening of the tunnel that led to the cavern. After we reached the entrance, we were waved on with smiles and cheers. It wasn't easy to leave our new family and friends but we continued into the dome of rock.

"It's good that Mahtagwaysoo decided to stay," I said.

"Now that Blackfeather won't be around to bother her," Abby added.

"He'd better stay away, I said. "Are you ready to do this?"

"I can't wait to get home and tell Grandmother Molly about Ki'kwa'jenu and Mahtagwaysoo," Abby said. We stood by the stone altar. I held her hand and Abby recited the ritual.

After the words were spoken, I wondered when we were. "I wish we had some way to know where we've landed."

"You mean *when* we landed. Sorry, Charlie, no flashing lights here. Come on, let's get home." We walked toward the bright light at the end of the tunnel.

Too Far
Chapter 19

We followed the path to Grandmother Molly's village. It was hard going. Many trees had been blown down across the trail. The spirit of the north wind, Kabibonokka, had been busy. The path looked like it hadn't been used for some time. We found a canoe under a pile of brush, but it wasn't the one we had left. Littered with layers of fallen leaves from many seasons before, it looked like it hadn't been disturbed for some time. Abby and I paddled across the stream. When we got to the village's courtyard where the celebrations and communal feasts had been held, there was no sign of life. There were fallen tree limbs here and there, and no one had bothered to rake up the yard. Molly's cabin looked like it had been abandoned for some years. There was a young birch tree growing up between the thick planks that formed her front steps. One of her window screens was hanging down off the sill, leaves plastering the glass and hiding what must have been cracks and missing pieces.

"This doesn't look good, Charlie. Where is everyone?" As she said that, Abby's brow frowned.

"Beats me," I said. "It looks like no one's been around for some time."

"Grandmother Molly never let her place look like this. It's like she isn't even here anymore."

"I'm sure she's not too far away," I said, trying to put a hopeful twist to things.

Hey, I see smoke above those trees," Abby pointed out.

"Where? I don't see anything," I said. "Wait, you mean over there?" I pointed to some tall trees that were beyond the courtyard.

"Let's check it out," Abby said, and we headed off to see what was there. A small shack came into view, white smoke snaking away from the stovepipe that stuck through the roof at an angle, painting sinuous white stripes that formed layers of haze on this calm morning.

An old man was sitting in a rocking chair on the front porch, reading. It was Hiram.

"Finally, you return. It is good to see you," Hiram said from the chair. "Forgive my manners, but it's difficult to stand up, so I don't follow ceremony anymore. Come up." Abby and I walked up the steps to a porch that overlooked a set of rapids.

"Hiram, what happened? Where is everyone?" I asked.

"Where's Grandmother Molly?" From the trembling in her voice, I sensed that Abby already knew the answer.

"You have been gone a long time," Hiram said. He had aged overnight; his pure white hair cascaded over his shoulders. His face, once smooth like a water worn stone, was now deeply furrowed in all directions. His ear lobes had elongated and hung down almost to his collar.

"No, we haven't," Abby asserted. "It's been only a couple of days, but it looks like no one's been here for years! There's a tree growing through Grandmother Molly's porch!"

"You're right about that," Hiram replied. "The last time you were here was nearly twenty years ago."

"Twenty years?" Abby and I said at the same time. "How could that happen?" she asked.

"You have come too far," Hiram said. "Something must have gone wrong in the cavern to put you this far off course."

"Where's Grandmother Molly?" Abby asked him again, dropping her voice to her most serious tone. She should have been sitting beside him in one of the rocking chairs or maybe sweeping her porch. "And why are you not in her cabin with her?" Abby missed that there was just one rocking chair on the porch now, or she guessed what had happened.

He hesitated for a moment. "She waited for you to return as long as she could. One day the Great Spirit came for her." Abby burst into tears, seeking comfort in my open arms. She didn't seem to realize that we were in just one of an infinite number of futures from any given point in time.

"I couldn't live in her cabin," Hi said. "There was too much of her still there. I kept waiting for her to walk through her front door"

"How?" Abby asked, drying her eyes.

"I found her at the spring one morning, leaning against a tree there. She had gone out to collect some plants along the river and must have needed a rest." Hiram explained. "She looked like she sat down for a nap, her back against an old yellow birch. There was such a peaceful look on her face. I carved her bear name on the tree where she last saw our world. I'm glad it happened in the woods and not in a place empty of what she loved so much."

Tears filled her eyes again; I took Abby's hand. "That's only one possible future, Abby. There is an infinite number of others. We must have made some mistake in the cavern," I said. "Can this be fixed?"

"I don't know," Hiram said. "You'll have to go back to the cavern and try again. Sometimes the spirits play games with us, and sometimes they don't pay attention when you need them the most."

"Not another trip," Abby said. "Hiram, show me the tree."

"We don't have time," I explained. "We need to do this now."

"He's right, Abby," Hiram said. "You took a wrong turn. Hand me that glass of water, would you?" He pointed to a glass on the kitchen table. I brought it over to him.

Hiram emptied the glass, and then put it on the little table beside him. "Where is everyone else?" I asked.

"The Company cut down all the old forests. There was no more game, no more fish, and the air has become so hazy all the time. It smells pretty bad most days, too. The villagers all moved away one by one. There are very few songbirds each spring. I heard only one yesterday, and not a peep this morning. The summers are much warmer, too, and maple sap season has been cut in half. Our gardens don't grow the way they used to. Frosts can happen late in June and early in August," Hiram sighed. "And now there's another great war in Europe." *This is the future my children could face*, I thought. The frustrating thing was that there was nothing I could do about it now. It was too late for this timeline, but maybe when we got back, we could figure out how to stop this future from happening.

"Are there any supplies here?" I asked. "We're almost out of provisions." My stomach was beginning to growl, protesting the meager meals the day before.

"Sure, Charlie, there are some in the pantry inside. Take what you need. I can resupply from the food bank when I get into town next week. When will you be going back to the Skull Cave?" Hiram asked.

"I think we should get something to eat, re-supply and return this afternoon," I said, "while there's still plenty of light."

"No Charlie, I can't. Let's start at first light tomorrow. Please?" Abby begged. I'm exhausted."

"Yeah, okay, I'm really tired, too," I said. "I don't think an overnight is going to hurt anything. Is the bunkhouse available?"

"You can stay in the one over there," Hiram said, pointing in the direction of another building hidden behind some trees. "Come by for dinner," he invited, reaching up and grabbing his fishing rod. "Perch are biting like crazy. We'll have a nice feed tonight if I can find some worms." He grabbed his staff in one hand, and took his alder fishing pole with the other. We stared after Hiram, hobbling off to his favorite perch hole just around the river bend.

"You know who'll be really glad to see us when we return don't you?" Abby asked. In order to get to the right time, we had to return to the cavern and briefly return to Blackfeather's time. Making that trip should reset whatever had gone wrong, and Abby could try again to get us to the right time stream. But while we were there, even for a short time, there was a huge risk of running into Blackfeather. Abby insisted that we did have to check to see if we did make it back to the right time, and that meant scouting out the village. Apparently, Grandmother Molly had given her strict instructions about how not to get lost in the river of time.

"I'm not worried about running into Blackfeather, though. I have you to watch out for me, right?" I asked her.

"If I have to wrestle Blackfeather, all bets are off. I don't think I'd win a match with that guy," Abby said. "If it hadn't been for your south wind, we'd be in a lot of trouble."

Abby and I headed to the bunkhouse. We unpacked our bedrolls, but welcomed the covered mattresses on real springs, one of the more thoughtful gestures of the Company. I wondered if we could defend ourselves against an angry Blackfeather when we got back to his village. He might be sore from the fallen oak branch, or he might be upset with me for defeating him at the challenge.

Hiram brought back dozens of white perch fillets. Abby and I gathered some acorns the squirrels missed the last fall, and she made a coarse flour to drag the fillets through before dropping them in the pan.

We feasted on fish with crispy potatoes and wild onions, fried over the fire.

"Tell me what happened with Blackfeather," Hiram said. Abby told him about the ceremony with Ki'kwa'jenu, the owl, and how he chased us to the cavern.

"You don't always come back to the same time you leave from, do you?" Hiram asked.

"No, we don't," I said. "Sometimes it's too far forward or too far back. The spirits don't always listen."

"I suppose," Hiram said, "you could end up practically in a bear's mouth or you could run into Blackfeather, alive and looking for revenge for losing another bride to be."

"What I have trouble understanding is how can you pull Blackfeather from his own time, put him into another time in the future, and still find him back in his own time as if he had never left," Hiram wondered.

"There are an infinite number of futures," Abby said. "Blackfeather will always exist in his own times, whichever ones those may be. Charlie's right. We've ended up in one of an infinite number of futures." *Wonderful*, I thought. *Just what we had talked about. Traveling like this is way too confusing for me.*

The next morning, Abby and I were off at first light. Abby was ready to go before I was, and I found her waiting impatiently by the fire pit. We said good-bye to Hiram.

"I can't wait to meet your younger self when we get back to the right time," I said to him.

"Just don't tell me how lame my hip has become," Hiram said. "I'd rather not know any details of this visit so I can continue to believe I'm indestructible."

"You wouldn't believe the story anyway, right?" I said.

"You're right, Charlie, I wouldn't even want to."

We slung our pack baskets over our shoulders and headed down the path to the canoe. The day started off with a hazy sky that nearly obscured the sun and a strong sulfur stink from the mill. Hiram was right. There were no songbirds. We hiked for a while and met no one on the trip, passing by only one log cabin that perched on the very edge of the riverbank. Years of heavy rains and snow melt had eroded the river's edge so much that the camp, originally a hundred feet away from the water, was about to topple into it.

"Isn't that Split Rock ahead?" Abby asked.

"I think so, but something doesn't look right. Something's missing," I said.

Then I could see what was different. The giant old cedar that had grown between the rocks forever had been downed in the last great windstorm, snapping off twenty feet above us.

"That must have been some south wind. Know anything about that, Charlie?" Abby asked.

"No, really, I don't. Nope, not at all. I hope I'm not going to be blamed every time Sowanakik decides to blow over a tree," I smiled.

We walked by the cedar's ragged stub and came to the downed top. It had landed right beside the trail. The old raven's nest was woven into the branches.

"Look," I pointed. "See something shining on the side?" There were pieces of colored glass here and there between the twigs, a popular décor when it comes to ravens' nests like this one. I was about to take it from the tightly woven nest.

"No, Charlie, don't touch it!" she screamed.

"But why not?" I asked, stopping in my tracks.

"We shouldn't upset this time stream by taking it back with us," Abby warned. "There is already one around Nolka's neck, and one in each time stream. It might cause problems if there were suddenly two or none at all."

"We should just leave it here?" I asked.

"We should. It might be right here when we return in the right time stream," Abby suggested. We put the crystal back in the fallen nest and gave Raven our thanks. We trekked on, back to Skull Cave.

Whenever I looked behind us, I could see a pair of black wings following at a distance. It seemed that Ki'kwa'jenu's power in our present wasn't very strong.

"Abby," I said.

"What?" She stopped abruptly, and I almost toppled into her.

"Ki'kwa'jenu is following us," I reported.

"Let me know if the black wings get any closer, okay?"

We trudged on to Skull Cave. Abby led the way. After a few hours' hike over the glacial boulder field and another slippery trip under the waterfall, we were at the opening of Skull Cave.

The ritual in the cavern went smoothly. The one thing we had to do again was to check to see when we arrived. We went through this process when we first started and made a couple of wrong turns. This time, we'd have to see if the village was still there, and then we'd need to confirm if we arrived right after the time when we left. At first we thought the only way to be sure, was to go all the way back to Nicatou. But if there were another time to come back, I would bury something along the trail or scratch a mark in a rock. But would that really be a guarantee that we were okay? Grandmother Molly explained that if we didn't come back and be sure the time was right, the spirits might be confused and send us off to another place in time's river. We didn't want to get lost in the current.

We walked to the cave's opening. We could see the village below us, and we could see Gray Wolf. "I think that looks good," I said, using the spy glass to survey the area.

"I hope so. Do you see Moosis or Mahtagwaysoo? Maybe Nolka?"

I raised the glass again. "There's Moosis, over by the firewood pile, practicing with his bow and arrow." I handed the glass to Abby. "I didn't see Little Rabbit, but Nolka is talking with Gray Wolf. There's no sign of Blackfeather." She handed the glass back to me.

"Shouldn't we go down to ask about Blackfeather? There's no sign of him."

"I don't think we need to take that chance," I said. I raised the spy glass once more. "Everything looks good from here. But I don't see his hut. See the opening where it used to be?" I handed the glass back to her.

"You're right," she said. "Blackfeather's hut is gone, and it looks like it was recently removed. I can still see where the poles were jammed into the ground. Let's try again to get back to Nicatou and Grandmother Molly.

"We can't check everything. Let's get back to Nicatou. We have the raven's nest to look for, so let's get a move on." I put the spy glass back in its case in my pocket. We went back into the cavern and went through the ceremony one more time.

Chesuncook Village
Chapter 20

Abby and I walked into the circle of light at the end of the tunnel. It was a bright May afternoon. I could see the smokestacks of the mill and the lakes and rivers below full of pulpwood and saw logs. Somehow, the evidence of Man's ability to strip his environment of anything valuable, including its natural ability to regenerate, was a comfort. We were home.

The hike back to Split Rock and beyond seemed easier this time. We had been back and forth now several times. Just ahead I could see where the raven's nest might have been. As we walked closer, I was positive that it was the right place, and there on the ground was the nest, having been tossed from a crashing tree top once swaying in the wind.

"I don't see the crystal," I said. We looked through the branches, the mud packs, the bits of colored glass.

"Here!" she shouted as she pulled the crystal, intact, out from the tangle of a root and branch mud daubed nest.

"What should we do with it?" I asked.

"Grandmother Molly should have it. After all, it belonged to her sister." We continued the hike home.

When we arrived in Molly's village, we were welcomed by everyone we passed.

There she was, weeding the peas with her hoe. Abby dropped her pack and ran to Awasosqua, wrapping her arms around her as she nearly knocked her over.

"You're back," Molly cried, as she dropped the hoe. "I hoped it would be soon." They embraced a moment, neither saying a word. "Everything is well? Molly looked my way. "I don't see Mahtagwaysoo."

"She decided to stay," I reported.

"And Blackfeather is gone," Abby said. "Twice."

"Twice?" Molly asked.

"We'll tell you about it over a cup of tea," Abby answered. "Where's Hiram?"

"Stubborn as ever, that old coot. He's fishing again," Molly sighed. "We might not have much of a garden this summer, but we will have lots and lots of dried fish this winter."

We followed Molly to the cabin and settled down with stories and tea. After Hiram returned with a string of perch, we shared the story of Ki'kwa'jenu and Blackfeather being one and the same. Abby described my battle with him at the challenge. Abby reached into her pocket and handed Nolka's crystal to Awasosqua.

"I'm so glad to have something my sister wore," she said as she put it on a lanyard and hung it from her neck. "And I'm glad to see you kept it apart from the amulet. Strange things can happen if they touch one another," she warned again. Abby started to remove the amulet from around her neck.

"No, Abby," Awasosqua said. "That belongs to you now. Who knows, maybe you'll need it someday?"

"I sure hope not," Abby said. "We nearly got lost more than once!"

We got caught up with the village news. All of Grandmother Molly's patients had recovered thanks to the medicinal plants we had brought back. The illness was finally gone from the village. Abby told them about the fight in the aerie and how brave she thought I was.

"I don't think the black wings will be bothering you anymore," Grandmother Molly observed. Then Hiram startled me.

"Two men came here looking for you," Hiram said. "It was a week ago, right Awasosqua?"

"Just about," she replied. "They were certainly city people by how they were dressed."

"What did they want?" I asked.

"They said that Caleb sent them and that you were to go with them to meet him in Bangor," Hiram paused.

"There's more," Grandmother Molly said. "They told us your

father was on his way to Thomaston State Prison. Seems he got picked up by the revenooers."

"Oh no! Is it safe to go home?" I asked.

"We think so, right Hiram?" Grandmother Molly asked.

"It probably is. That stuff about Thomaston just isn't true," Hiram said. "They were too citified to have been sent by Caleb. Besides, Thomaston is state, not federal."

"What did you tell them?" I asked.

"I told them you had been here but left for Bangor the day after you arrived. I told them you had had enough of the moonshine business and were running away for a better, safer life." He stopped to collect his thoughts. "And that you and Abby had eloped."

"Oh, Hiram, you didn't!" said Abby. "What if this gets back to my aunt?"

"I don't think you have to worry, Abby," he said. "They weren't from Caleb and weren't staying in the Village. They were looking for you for another reason."

"They weren't sent by my father?" I wanted to confirm.

"That's the size of it," Hiram said. "I think the Boston gang is still sore about the last time. They seemed hot to get their hands on you."

"But why Charlie?" Abby asked. "Why not Caleb?"

"Because they probably wanted to kidnap me for a nice big ransom from Father," I said. "And that would have been paid in a lot of Tanglefoot over a long period of time."

"You might want to be looking over your shoulder for a while," Grandmother Molly said.

"Don't worry," I said. "I've been watching for black wings for a long time, so no problem looking for a couple of goons."

"You still need to be careful," Abby cautioned.

"I'll be careful. Sowanakik travels with me." The south wind had saved the day more than once. "Are you coming back to the Village?" I asked Hiram.

"That's up to Awasosqua," he replied and smiled in her direction.

"And that depends on how many fish you catch!" she chuckled. With that, we all had a good laugh. In the morning we hugged goodbye and started on the trail to the river to make our way home. Finally, I thought, as I looked over my shoulder. It had been a long time.

We uncovered our canoe. I was still looking for something out of place but nothing came up. We poled upstream along the riverbank and carried our gear around the rapids. When we came to a bend in the river, we could see a horse and wagon beside a cook fire. It would be lunchtime for the river drivers soon, and maybe we could hitch a ride upriver.

"Any chance we could catch a ride with you to the Dam?" I asked. We loaded the canoe and our gear into the wagon, and soon the horses were straining to pull us up Little Eddy Hill toward Chesuncook Dam.

"This road hasn't gotten any smoother," I complained, grasping the wagon's side.

"I thought the Company was going to fix it?" Abby asked.

"Hard tellin', not knowin'," the driver answered. Abby was sitting with her back against his seat. "But I did hear the Company is plannin' to push the road from the Dam all the way to Millinocket." That would have to be an improvement.

The driver turned his attention to his team, urging the horses up the rise and letting loose a long, brown stream of tobacco juice, some dribbling into his stained beard. In a moment, he turned back, this time to me. I was propped up in the corner.

"Sorry to hear about your father," he said. "Two men came looking for you." He turned back to his team, not waiting for a response. We clattered over the rough, rocky road. The bouncing around made the tobacco juice stream more challenging to avoid.

"I've got to move over there," I said to Abby. She grabbed a duffle and laid it out for me to lean against. I moved over, further away from the occasional brown stream shooting from the driver's mouth.

"Okay, this is better," I said as I settled against a green army canvas duffle bag filled with pots and pans as the poking in my back suggested. A half hour later we passed the driving camps on Ripogenus Lake. Abby and I rode quietly. Everything we wanted to talk about, our trip, what the heck was going on with Father, we had to wait until we were alone. I thought the two strangers looking for me were spreading a story to make their search for me seem more innocent than it really was.

We turned down the Chesuncook Dam road, the last mile of a dusty trip. Everything looked the same. The Boom House on the rise had smoke drifting from the chimney, suggesting there was something good cooking in the stove. I was starving. When the wagon pulled up to the barn, it was time to climb down and unload.

"Where's the canoe going?" Abby asked. I was untying the rope that held it fast to the wagon. After he unhitched the horses and brought them into the stable, the driver went in to see the payroll clerk. He'd pocket his season's pay and spend it all in a week's time in Bangor speakeasys.

"We'll put it inside the barn over there," I pointed. Abby was waiting to grab the canoe's bow as I slid it from the wagon. We carried the canoe into the open barn where we slid it into an empty slot in a rack holding several others. "You'd think the Company was in the canoe business," I said.

"They'll all be out of here in a few weeks when the timber cruisers come," Abby said. Company men would travel the rivers and streams, making note of ponds, small creeks that could be dammed to flush a few logs through, ridges of tall spruce, fir and pine. Most of the big pine was gone, and we were now into second and third growth cycles from when men first started cutting in 1830.

"How long have we been gone?" I asked.

"I'm pretty sure it's been a week," Abby said.

"Seems longer," I said.

"Two days to get there, two days to get back here. We stayed over two nights when we were way back, and one night with Grandmother Molly, last night. That makes seven."

We started to carry our gear to the docks after unloading everything from the wagon.

"Let's see if we can find a newspaper." I put my pack down beside the catwalk leading to the float but far enough away to keep it dry from the waves.

"We could get something to eat while we wait for the *Twilight*," Abby suggested. "I'm starving. Maybe we'll hear some great gossip from Cookee."

"I was just thinking," I said.

"About?" she asked.

"If we are in the wrong time stream, then is it a bad thing? Do we have a choice to go back to the petroglyphs and try again, or not?"

"I don't know for sure. We probably could. We'd have to go back to see Molly and Hiram and see what they think. But let's get a paper first. Maybe we are in the right time stream," Molly said.

The sun disappeared and a white curtain of rain was heading right for us. We grabbed a nearby canvas from the dock's gear box, threw it over our duffels and hurried up the hill to the Boom House. The porch benches were empty with the men still out to work. I opened the door just as the curtain of rain hit.

"Darn squalls," Cookee said. "Had to close that there door four times already this morning. Must be racing along one of those Canadian Clippers sailing by." Sometimes we'd get one rain squall, then the sun, and then another blow ten minutes later. It was if the weather didn't know what to do. "How's your father doing?" Cookee asked. "He hasn't stopped in for a while."

"We're headed up the lake now when he gets in. Could we get some lunch?" I asked.

We had pot roast, potatoes and carrots, bread right out of the oven, iced tea and some cookies for dessert. I was stuffed.

"Is there a recent paper?" I asked Cookee.

"I lit the stove this morning with the last one. Mail should be coming in a few hours, I think. Should be one there. Not much news if ya ask me."

We thanked Cookee and headed out to the porch. The sky had lightened. We sat at the checker corner to wait for the boat.

"I keep wondering who's going to be on the boat," I said.

"I don't think you'll have to wait long to find out," she said. "There's the boat now."

I turned to see the *Twilight* coming down the lake. Behind her, another white curtain of rain overtook her, engulfing the boat. But the storm was on a different track, and soon her brilliant white bow came through the curtain heading through the whitecaps toward the pier.

"She had to surf down all those swells," I said. The north wind was pretty strong, blowing the foam straight off the peaking waves, some of which topped three feet.

"It won't be much fun heading into that," Abby said. "Maybe we'll have to stay until things calm down."

"I hope not," I said. "I want to get home, but first I want to hear what's been going on."

"You'll probably hear it from Uncle Amos. I can see his pipe from here," Abby said. The *Twilight* came closer to the pier and floating dock where we were soon standing to grab her lines. Standing on the dock was like balancing on the surface of a giant bowl of Jell-O.

Amos was steering. That was unusual. Father rarely gave up the helm. Louis threw me the stern rope. I snagged it around the cleat and pulled tight. Amos had put her in reverse and was giving the engine some gas to help stop the forward motion. Meanwhile, Louis scrambled to the bow to throw Abby that line. The bottom half of my pants were soaking wet.

"Charlie, been wondering where you got lost at," Louis smiled. "'Bout time you got back. It's been more than two weeks now. We were going to go look for you." He turned to open one of the Moxie-not Moxie crates and fished out a bottle of Tanglefoot. "Cookee is going to be looking for this." He smiled and slid the bottle into his jacket pocket.

I didn't tell him we had been gone a longer time than he figured. I couldn't tell him that we weren't lost anywhere here….just in the river of time. He wouldn't have believed me.

"Like the new labels?" Louis asked, reaching for a second bottle for delivery to the kitchen. He held it up for me to see. 'Nighthawk Distillery' was printed in black ink on a white label. Black wings of the Nighthawk were prominent in the background.

"No more Moxie bottles?" I asked.

"Just for the cases that were easiest for the deputies to inspect," he said. "Probably eight or ten along the front of the load. Those are marked with a black star. Aren't the labels great?" He beamed with pride.

Louis' wife, Anna, had come to the Nighthawk, a house of ill repute I should say, and the first day she arrived Louis stopped in. He ended the day rescuing her, marrying her, and whisking her away to our village. He probably saved her life. She was an accomplished seamstress and now an artist it would appear. I had no response, just nodded my head wondering if I would ever see those black wings as a creative company design the way Louis did.

"Why so little Tanglefoot?" I asked. The boat was only half loaded. There were no trucks waiting for it at the pier. "What's happened?"

"Got a new business," Father said, crawling out of engine room and onto the boat deck. I froze. His stubby cigar danced around the edges of his mouth, seeming to migrate from one side to the other as it were a live thing.

"I keep hearing you're on your way to Thomaston," I said. "What the heck is going on?"

"Oh, don't listen to that crap," Father said. "Folks don't know what they're talking about. Yes, I did get a little visit from the revenooers, but we were ready for them. We hid the product under the manure pile. Amos and Louis worked all night breaking down the stills and hiding the parts here and there." He paused. "I heard the Boston gang was looking for you." He looked at me. "You got that look, Charlie," he warned. My mouth must have been open. I looked over to Abby. By this time, a chain of men formed and woodsmen's duffels were passed from one to the other until they ended up in the back of a little wagon that had just backed down to the pier. On it were gray sacks of mail ready to go upriver, and crates of food plus some longer looking crates I didn't recognize until much later. Soon, the cargo destined for the Village was loaded into the boat.

"What's the new business?" I asked, now getting a little more worried than I was when the Nighthawk was after us. At least we were in the right time stream, I hoped.

"Running guns," Louis whispered.

"And a few select fugitives," Father replied, even quieter. Then he looked at the lake. "We're not going back in that," he shouted to Amos and Louis above a sudden gust, gesturing to the storm front. "Let's plan to stay here tonight. I'll find us some bunks." Father walked down the float to the path leading to the Boom House.

I sighed and followed him up the path along the refueling pipes. I was looking forward to another game of checkers with Abby, but while she beat me hands down, I was thinking of making deals with the Devil. That was indeed Father. We really are home and at the right time.

About the Author

B.W. Edwards spent summers at Chesuncook Village as a child. He lives and writes in northern Maine and North Carolina.